To choose an obscure character from an obscu
requires a uniquely imaginative mind and also
places, and people. In this charming story Estill
of humor that distinguished his life. It is a thor
many heroes of the first-century church, making ....auer while showing their
relationship to each other. Dr. Jones beautifully painted a picture of these people and of the time and
culture into which the first Christian churches were born.

—*Mary Etta Sanders, former teacher, and Drayton Sanders, physician*

Estill Jones became my mentor and senior minister in 1972 at Dogwood Hills Baptist Church in East Point, Ga. Having served as a seminary professor with a focus on New Testament Greek, his passion and expertise with Greek surfaced frequently in his preaching and teaching. This was especially true when a group of Baptist friends started meeting with monks at the Monastery of the Holy Spirit to translate the Greek New Testament into English and engage in spirited conversation. When I learned about Estill's retelling of Onesimus' story, I remembered that Philemon was one of the New Testament books we translated. I can still sense Estill's excitement in talking about the many nuances of the story more than 40 years ago. In *Onesimus: A Slave's Pathway to True Freedom*, Estill brings his knowledge of New Testament Greek, his steadfast faith, and keen imagination to create a wonderful narrative of Onesimus' life. In the process he weaves the development of the early church and some of the key players in the Jesus movement into the story. I can picture Estill's delight in telling the story that is now part of his legacy. May God bless you as you read the story told in a fresh and insightful way and perhaps experience a new sense of freedom in Christ for yourself.

—*T. Lee Stephens, former Episcopal priest*

Never have I been more aware of the mountain of knowledge an author of historical fiction must have to write such an engaging story as this. Estill Jones wrote with the depth and attention to detail of a serious biblical scholar, the imagination and creativity of a lecturer and preacher, the understanding of human nature that came from being a counselor and chaplain, and the sensitivity of someone who devoted himself to his wife and children. His easy use of more current vocabulary, without drawing attention to it, draws the reader into a very old story about the meaning of freedom that has relevance even now.

—*Susan G. Broome, former archivist*

Estill and Violet Jones first became friends to my wife Sue and me in the 1980s when he took the job as seminary pastor at the Southern Baptist Theological Seminary. I discovered he was an astute New Testament scholar; a thoughtful and compassionate preacher; and caring nurturer of students, faculty, and staff. His gifts and extensive experience as a pastor, seminary professor, and devoted church person in retirement are evident in this delightful novel drawn from the biblical book of Philemon. Dr. Jones wove a geographical, cultural, and ethical understanding into this story of redemption of a Roman slave, Onesimus, in the first century. It is delightful to read and enormously informative as one imagines the travels, culture, and issues of the churches founded by the Apostle Paul. Each reader will have a new understanding of the power of the gospel in human reconciliation.

—*Larry L. McSwain, former professor and associate theology dean*

I suspect many people wonder about the stories that provide the background to the Apostle Paul's epistles. In his book, Estill Jones offers an imaginative behind-the-scenes look at the cast of characters in the shortest of those letters: Philemon. Using his vast knowledge of scripture, culture and tradition, he weaves a story describing the persistence of Paul, the ultimate graciousness of Archippus, and the faith of Onesimus. It's a story of freedom freely told by one who was not afraid to take the risk of creating conversations and emotions that exceed the limits of the biblical text. This is a story for all who have wondered how Onesimus became a slave, how he escaped from slavery, and how he was received when he returned to face Archippus. Dr. Jones offers us his imaginative answers. To paraphrase a portion of Paul's letter: "I have received much joy and encouragement from your thoughtfulness and creativity [love]; may the hearts of the saint be refreshed through you, my brother" (Philemon 7).

—*Michael Catlett, former pastor*

The first time I ever heard about Estill Jones came through his nickname as a professor. The students dubbed him fondly "Pistol Pete." A positive and energetic reputation gathered around that nickname. I knew immediately I wanted to meet him. You can meet his creativity and sense of drama in the saga of Onesimus, an inspiring story of a slave's pathway to freedom. Important scholarly opinions hide behind this energetic drama, but you will be taken by the narrative and adventure of this scintillating story.

—*Peter Rhea Jones, former pastor and professor*

Estill Jones' first and only novel totally reflects who and what he was. It is a creative way to exegete and expand the biblical book of Philemon, enabling the reader to become well acquainted with a slave named Onesimus. Calling on his fertile imagination and his immense knowledge of the New Testament, Jones shares vivid insight into the social, economic, political, and religious cultures during the time when fledgling fellowships of believers were evolving into what became the Christian church. He makes living persons out of long-dead Jesus followers, and causes Onesimus to become a household name to many for whom he had only been a nodding acquaintance. While taking certain liberties with the account itself, it is clearly obvious the writer was intimately acquainted with the appropriate texts.

—*Floyd Roebuck, former pastor*

From the first page of this book I hear Estill Jones' voice in all its clarity. I recognize his approach: clear and to the point. His scholarship comes through in his descriptions of events, big and small, that shaped the formation of the Apostle Paul's world and led to the many letters Paul penned to the young churches of his world. In telling the story of Onesimus' struggle to survive, then thrive, Jones brings to life the people and cultures of the first century. He reminds us to not be satisfied with the life that other people choose for us. As we read about Onesimus, we see some of the issues facing Paul and other early Christians, issues we still grapple with today: respect for women, constructive use of power, compassion for humanity, and justice for the downtrodden of society. The story of a runaway slave, Onesimus, is told within the narrative of the early Christian landscape. Both slave and church are finding their way to come of age. This story will appeal to readers of different ages.

—*Joe W. Davis, former elementary school principal*

In an inspiring novel set during the time of St. Paul's ministry and based on the account of Onesimus in the New Testament Book of Philemon, Estill Jones weaves Onesimus' yearning for freedom in with the gospel message preached by Paul. The novel is reminiscent of *The Robe* by Lloyd C. Douglas, although much shorter. Jones' background as a New Testament scholar is evident in this powerful story of the challenges of living the Christian life and starting new churches during early Christian times.

—*Merrill Davies, author of four historical novels*

Based on Paul's letter to Philemon, *Onesimus: A Slave's Pathway to True Freedom* is a scripturally inspired and yet vividly imagined story of the life of a young boy who is sold into slavery and then experiences the changing powers of redemption—ultimately leading to the true freedom for which he seeks. Readers young and old will find this to be a compelling tale.

—*Betty Stanley, former upper elementary teacher*

Onesimus is given a history: his parents are killed, and he is sold into slavery. But he yearns for the freedom he once knew. Young adult readers, and even older adults who enjoy novels based on biblical characters, will enjoy traveling with Onesimus on his pathway to freedom.

—*Ruth T. Rowell, musician and Christian educator*

Estill Jones, an esteemed Baptist ethicist of the 1950s, combined his biblical scholarship and historical expertise to give the reader of *Onesimus: A Slave's Pathway to True Freedom* a believable account of a bitter young slave who runs away from his master, becomes a follower of Jesus, and then returns to his slave owner. Will he be accepted or made to face the traditional punishment meted out to runaway slaves?

—*Lynelle Mason, author of eight books, including five novels*

In this imaginative retelling of the story of Onesimus and Archippus, based on the Book of Philemon, Estill Jones does a wonderful job of transporting us to the Lycus Valley and sketching some memorable characters whose words and actions give added texture to Paul's letter to Philemon. Ultimately, this book illustrates the transformative power of the Christian faith. It will serve both lay and clergy alike. Lay readers will learn the value of "reading between the lines," and clergy will learn again the importance of good storytelling.

—*Bill Ireland, former pastor*

A cogent, winsome account of Paul's critical role in setting a slave free for Christian ministry. . . While calling on his thorough grasp of Paul's life and letters, J. Estill Jones also used his gift for creative conjecture about the enslavement, escape, conversion, romance, marriage, and ministry of Onesimus. I knew Dr. Jones was a noted scholar, but now I marvel at his knack for bringing vivid, real-life events alive. Oh Estill, you *can* tell a tale!

—*Dan Whitaker, former pastor*

I have always been disappointed with St. Paul's reluctance to condemn the institution of slavery, but as I read *Onesimus: A Slave's Pathway to True Freedom*, I became angry and upset with Paul. Estill Jones wanted readers to respond to the characters in scripture as real people. Like a caring pastor and teacher, he wove biblical scholarship and imaginative storytelling to help us feel the hope of the gospel.

—*Brett Younger, pastor and author*

Philemon and Onesimus take on new life when seen through the eyes of Estill Jones' vivid imagination. It is amazing how much detail he wove into this brief novel. The writing style is such that readers of different ages can follow the story Jones painted. But those readers familiar with the New Testament, Paul, and Paul's writings will better identify and understand the intricate details Jones included. Thank you, Estill, for the book, your scholarship, your imagination, your Christian commitment, and your friendship.

—*Joanne Nimmons, former media specialist, and Billy Nimmons, former pastor*

Drawing on his extensive knowledge of Paul's letters and their historical and cultural background, New Testament professor and pastor Estill Jones used his educated imagination to provide a fascinating story of a little-known character of the New Testament—Onesimus the runaway slave. The book is informative, enjoyable, and stimulating.

—*Joe Baskin, former professor of religion*

Estill Jones used his great knowledge of scripture and his creative writing skills to craft a compelling story of the runaway slave, Onesimus. Each page brings a delightful twist to the narrative as Jones wove familiar biblical characters such as Paul, Timothy, Luke, Aristarchus, and Philemon into the life journey of Onesimus. Estill's writing made the story come to life.

—*Larry Flanagan, former minister of music*

Estill Jones wove the little we know about Onesimus into the vast tapestry of the Pauline letters. The result is a creative and compelling pilgrimage of a young escaped slave. If you enjoy historical fiction, you will love the way Dr. Jones brought to life the work of Paul through Onesimus' story.

—*Jonathan Barlow, pastor*

In this biblical novel. Estill Jones repeats his challenge to the "free in Jesus" to be a positive example to those who are shackled by burdens of sin and therefore without the freedom that comes with the reception of God's love and grace. He challenges those who receive this freedom to be responsible in living both the physical and spiritual life.

—*Jimmy Hatcher, former pastor and director of missions*

Onesimus
A Slave's Pathway to True Freedom
J. Estill Jones

© 2018
Published in the United States by Nurturing Faith Inc., Macon GA,
www.nurturingfaith.net.

Library of Congress Cataloging-in-Publication Data is available.

ISBN 978-1-63528-057-9

All rights reserved. Printed in the United States of America

Foreword

His name meant "Profitable." However, Archippus did not consider this to be the case with his slave Onesimus. Rather, the young man appeared to keep the entire household in turmoil. "Why did I ever call you Onesimus? You have been anything but profitable to me. I'm tempted to sell you—if I could get a good price."

As an enthusiastic, lively, healthy teenager and young adult between the ages of 15 and 21, Onesimus sneaked out with young Julius under his care, took a horse without permission, was accused of thievery for taking fruit (as many teenagers, he was obsessed with food!), and finally escaped.

Of course, the story doesn't end there. In this historical fiction, Dad (aka Dr. Jones, J. Estill, Pistol Pete, Bud, Uncle Estill) considers the life of a young man who never gives up hope of regaining his freedom from slavery, while in the process gaining freedom of the soul, heart and mind, and maturing into a committed Christian leader.

Throughout the story, Onesimus' path to spiritual freedom is influenced by many individuals, including Paul, characterized by those surrounding him as "fiery, independent, committed." Onesimus is grateful to be referred to as Paul's "faithful and beloved brother" and "son in the faith." Numerous details of the early church are presented, along with various characters whose ministry helped shape it.

In addition to telling the story of Onesimus, Dad wove a number of cultural and historical themes of the day: the unjust nature of slavery, political and legal issues, religious differences, discrimination, philosophy, ethics, crime, economics, love, leadership roles of women, marital relationships, education, career aspirations, and adolescent inquiry. Sound current?

We don't know when Dad wrote this book. Maybe it was during our own teen years, perhaps in the 1940s after completing his dissertation on *Philemon*, or even more recently. We know that he began each day at the kitchen table, reading his Greek New Testament and writing. Possibly he penned it then. His love of scriptures, normal wit, creative twists and turns, storytelling skill, and theological insights are all evident as one reads the book. No doubt, Onesimus would have enjoyed the story.

Although we do not know Dad's intended audience, we suspect it will appeal to various ages at every stage of Christian growth. We do know that several months before Dad passed away in 2017, we were discussing "something important," and he brought out *Onesimus of Laodicea*. The manuscript had been typed, probably on his old IBM Selectric typewriter (and with very few errors!). With that, we transferred the story to a Word document, submitted it, and a few days before he died he received notification that the book had been selected for publication. Dad was elated!

We feel sure Dad would want to dedicate the book to our mother, Violet ("VI"), his wife and biggest supporter for 70 years.

The Jones Children
Jack, Jean, and Judson

Who's Who

Alexander: escaped slave; befriended Onesimus in Ephesus
Apollos: Christian orator from Alexandria, Egypt
Apphia: wife of Philemon
Aquila: tentmaker; Christian leader in Ephesus
Archippus: landowner-businessman; purchased Onesimus
Aristarchus: companion of Paul's from Thessalonica
Astrallus: astrologer-seeker type
Barnabas: teacher-companion of Paul's from Antioch of Syria
Claudia: slave girl in the house of Archippus
Demetrius: shopkeeper in Ephesus; employed Onesimus
Epaphras: Paul's student; lectured in Laodicea on freedom
Epictetus: slave; questioned Christian teachers regarding freedom
Ezra: astrologer-seeker type
Gaius: companion of Paul's from Derbe
Hector: supervisor of slave boys and maids at the home of Archippus
Heraclides: friend of Paul; provided lodging and work for Onesimus in Tarsus
Hermes: slave; oversaw Onesimus after purchase by Archippus
John Mark: early teacher-companion of Paul's
Julius: son of Archippus
Justus: kitchen slave at the home of Archippus
Luke: physician; fellow minister with Paul
Lydia: Thyatira merchant of purple dyes and fabrics; Christian leader
Marcus: member of Archippus' household staff; accompanied Onesimus to Ephesus
Onesimus: young man from Lystra; sold into slavery after his parents' murders
Paul: leader of the Christian movement following his conversion
Philemon: friend to Archippus; leader of the Christian movement in Colossae
Poppae: slave in charge of the kitchen at Archippus' home
Porphyra: mother of Onesimus
Prisca: wife of Aquila
Prochurus: father of Onesimus
Rufus: friend to Aquilla and Prisca; son of Simon, the cross-bearer for Jesus
Timothy: young companion of Paul's
Tychicus: companion of Paul's; leader in the church at Ephesus

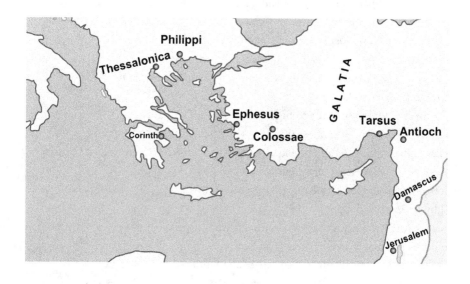

1

He remembered when and how. He was 15 years old and a normal boy, the only child of his parents. His father was a teacher in Lystra and helped to manage the unimposing jewelry shop near the center of town. His mother was in the shop most of the time. Occasionally Onesimus was allowed to make a sale. Most of the time he studied—or so it seemed to him. His father saw to that. Both father and son planned for him to attend the University of Tarsus, though neither looked forward to the necessary separation.

There were outings. Porphyra closed the shop one day a week. In the summer she prepared a picnic lunch and the family walked outside the city's area to a shady grove for an enjoyable holiday. Once after they had spread their blanket and the lunch on top of it they saw a snake slithering past. Porphyra screamed. Onesimus quickly pulled away, leaving the lunch for the slimy creature. Prochorus, as quickly, grabbed a stick and drove the snake away. Onesimus remembered his father's courage. The picnic continued.

Then there was the day it had seemed all of Lystra was on holiday. A strange teacher came to town. There were actually two of them: one they called Paul, the other Barnabas . . . Jews from Antioch in Syria. Onesimus and his parents did not witness the miracle, but they had known the lame man. Everyone in Lystra knew him. Amazingly, after being unable to stand alone for so many years, now he walked. Many in the crowd ahead called Paul and Barnabas gods—Hermes and Zeus. Soon a religious ceremony began: they were about to worship the strange teachers.

At this point Prochorus gently guided Porphrya and Onesimus off the beaten track and away from the mob. He knew about mobs. A few days later the mob attacked the two teachers and beat them severely. Prochorus, himself a teacher, did not appear to be concerned. But then he was not a religious man. Onesimus simply wondered that the lame man appeared to be healed.

The crisis came abruptly. On one of the mornings when Onesimus and his parents were in the shop a couple of ruffians came in. They were strangers and examined the merchandise, supposedly looking for an amethyst pendant. The wife or mistress of one had expressed a desire for it. When there seemed to be nothing to their liking they became abusive in tone. Soon they were threatening the owners.

"You must have some things under the counter we haven't seen. We want to see all of your stock."

"Sir, we do not have an amethyst pendant. You may find what you're looking for at another shop."

Prochorus spoke patiently. The visitors were impatient. One, the biggest and ugliest, moved behind the counter and began to finger the jewels. He placed several nice pieces in his bag. Prochorus objected and a struggle developed. The ruffian struck Prochorus to the floor and kicked him roughly. Porphyra, in a desperate attempt to save her husband, was also beaten to the floor. Only Onesimus stood to face the strangers.

He no longer liked to think about that day. He witnessed his parents beaten to death, the little shop robbed and vandalized. He bent over to tend his parents' wounds and was cruelly kicked.

"Wait—wait," spoke one of the attackers. "We can take this one and sell him. He's young and won't be much trouble."

With an evil leer he seized the boy by the arm and jerked him to the middle of the shop—what was left of it. Hastily the two ruffians drew the shades, as if the shop was closed, and left Porphyra and Prochorus behind the counter.

It was yet early and there were few people on the street. When the street was completely clear the three men walked out and closed the door. Onesimus was now between them as they made their way to the horses tied nearby. Roughly the young man was lifted to the horse's back and as roughly one of the two robbers mounted behind him. The other mounted his horse and the three rode out of Lystra on the west side of town. Onesimus, slightly built, struggled but was rudely cuffed about the head.

All that day they rode, coming to camp outside Iconium. There they bound Onesimus with cords around his wrists and ankles. They fed him—though he had no appetite, as he was sickened and crushed by the terror of the morning. Early the next morning they set out for Antioch. The road was winding and rough. Two days later they came to the outskirts of the city. One entered and looked around. There was to be a slave auction the next day. With threats and curses they prepared Onesimus for the sale. If he acted as more than a slave, they'd kill him.

Bound hand and foot, they took Onesimus to the slave block the next day. He was a likely-looking lad for his age—of normal height and slender. He spoke Greek as well as his native Lycaonian tongue. He might serve as a tutor or at least as a companion to a child. There were few buyers present. He was purchased by a man whom he afterwards learned to be Archippus. Gently but firmly his master led him away from the market and to his own animals.

The ride west was uneventful. Archippus was traveling with another slave to whom he entrusted Onesimus. Hermes was older—perhaps in his mid-20s. He appeared to obey, if not respect, Archippus, and he expected Onesimus to obey him.

"Get on the animal."

When the younger man hesitated, Hermes jerked his arm. Larger and much stronger, he controlled the situation. The slave owner did not seem to notice. They made camp at the close of the day, and Onesimus was secured so he could not escape.

Asia was a different province from Galatia. Onesimus had never been in Asia. Now, instead of the rough hill country and simple farmers and small-time tradesmen, the road leveled out and towns were more frequent and those who traveled were more prosperous. He might have responded more agreeably to the change in scenery if it had been in the company of his father. Snatched from the tiny shop, having seen his parents killed and left alone, he grieved both for them and for himself. Afraid, alone, and uncertain, he said nothing over the long miles except when addressed.

"Boy, when we get to the master's house you'll take orders from me. You'll say 'sir' when you address me. Try that: 'sir'."

Onesimus pretended not to hear. An arm reached out to get his attention. "I said that you were to address me as 'sir'."

Onesimus responded with little more than a whisper.

"Yes, sir."

Boiling now with resentment, anxious about the future, and feeling guilty about his inability to defend his parents, the young man rode wearily westward. Yet he could not close his eyes to the countryside.

The horsemen disturbed a herd of sheep, dark in color and—although Onesimus knew little about sheep—seemingly large and strong and woolly. Other flocks appeared, each under the supervision of a shepherd. He wondered aloud to himself if he, too, could be a shepherd and supposed that he could.

The group neared a town. Hermes identified it as Hierapolis. Becoming more talkative, but in an authoritarian manner and a sneering tone, he pointed southward.

"That's Colossae. These three cities are close neighbors and occasionally rivals. And there's the Lycus River. If you're a good boy, I'll take you fishing."

Resentment was yielding to hostility, and hostility to hatred. Yet Onesimus was struck by the beauty of the place. More travelers, more houses—and then he looked out on the broad Meander plane. The Lycus River, coming from its narrow gorge, watered it generously. This was Laodicea, an important center of commerce, 11 miles west of Colossae and 6 miles south of Hierapolis. He could see it—on a small plateau, just south of the river. Behind it, to the south and southwest, were snow-capped mountains. Later he learned their names: Salbakos and Kadmos. He would not dare ask Hermes about them. They reigned up at a large villa with stone construction, ample grounds, and nice landscaping.

Archippus approached and spoke kindly but clearly.

"Onesimus, eh? You will be profitable to me, alright. Just remember: You were once Onesimus of Lystra, but now you are Onesimus of Laodicea. Never forget that."

It was difficult to forget that. He was a slave to Archippus, under Hermes' authority.

2

"Up, up . . . to bed, to bed . . . out, out . . . go, go . . . work, work . . ."

Although the house in Lystra had not been so large and impressive, Onesimus at least had a spot he could call his own. In the slave quarters at Laodicea he barely had room for his cot or spot on the floor when another slave stole his cot. There was little or no privacy, rare silence, much movement, order or organization non-existent—just people and work all of the time.

Hermes saw to it that Onesimus was consigned to the stables. Onesimus thought it was the worst job in the household. The lad's father and mother had taught him responsibility, but he had responded to their appreciation. He received no appreciation from Hermes and rarely saw Archippus. He had little time for rest or recreation. Picnics were not the order of the day, or the week, or the month. In any event, few members of the household acted in a picnic mood. Slavery was anything but a picnic.

After a few months, which seemed like years, Archippus called for Onesimus to be brought from the stables to the house. There he talked with him.

"I know that you are resentful and hate your work and hate Hermes and hate me. I understand that, but that's just the way it is. I paid money for you. I'm feeding you. I expect to get my money's worth. I expect you to be profitable."

A momentary silence prompted the young man to speak.

"I have tried. I have obeyed. I have worked. I am not accustomed to cleaning stables."

"That's the reason I have brought you here. I think you will be more useful in the house. Indeed, when I purchased you I had this in mind. I want you to become a companion for Julius, my son."

Immediately Onesimus brightened. This would mean moving from the stable slave quarters to the main house. This would mean quiet and orderliness, eating at the table with Julius, enjoying the library with him.

"Julius is an alert, active nine-year-old. You will set a good example for him. You will help him with his school work. You may even go to his studies with him. I want you to speak only Greek with him—you speak excellent Greek.

Forget your native tongue. Make a new life for yourself. I have learned about the death of your parents, and I am sorry. What say we make the best of a bad situation? I will hold you responsible for Julius. He is my only son. You act like a responsible big brother."

The emphasis on "responsible" fell on ready ears. Onesimus understood. Of course, he resented his slavery. Perhaps he could gain his freedom. Perhaps he could escape. But for now, he would be responsible. He responded with appreciation to his owner.

"Thank you, sir. I will accept Julius as my nine-year-old brother."

About that time young Julius entered the room. His father introduced him to Onesimus, as Julius had not frequented the stables. At once the two were attracted to one another. Julius would have an older brother—a slave, to be sure. Onesimus would exchange his animal responsibility for human responsibility. Julius seemed excited.

"Come, Onesimus. Come see my room and your room."

Archippus smiled with satisfaction as the two boys left his presence.

The grand tour of the boy's room was short and somehow led through the room with its books and toys back toward the kitchen. It was apparent that Julius was a household favorite. News about his new relationship with Onesimus spread rapidly. By the time the boys reached the kitchen, a snack was spread. The kitchen slaves represented a different level of behavior. Onesimus met Poppae, who seemed to be in charge. She was an important person to know.

"Another mouth to feed? And a growing boy at that! Why doesn't the master add slaves instead of appetites?"

Onesimus welcomed the not-so-well-camouflaged humor. Younger slaves scurried around, preparing for the midday meal of lamb and herbs. One of the girls, about the age of Onesimus and named Claudia, nodded approvingly when she caught his name.

"Onesimus? He may be a profitable friend."

Onesimus was not blind or deaf or stupid. He sensed the beginning of a beautiful friendship.

For a time he was satisfied—as content as a slave in the household of Archippus might be. Julius was a ready pupil and kept the slave with him—or Onesimus kept Julius with him. Almost inseparable, the boys excited the friendliness of the slaves and freedmen—and on occasion provoked the jealousy of some. There was Hermes, for example, whose favorite target had somehow been removed from his clutches. When he saw Onesimus now he was clean and well dressed as a household slave. Hermes dared not accost him personally but began to plot against him.

He began to talk with his friend Hector, supervisor of the maids and boys who kept the house clean and orderly, about Onesimus.

"That young fellow needs to be watched. He's sneaky. To be sure, he gave us no trouble on the road from Lystra. But he gave me nothing but trouble when we arrived. He complained about his work—the dirt and the stench. He had to be constantly prodded to get the stables clean. And on occasion he proved to be too friendly with the young men . . . know what I mean?"

Of course, Hector knew what Hermes implied. It was a familiar problem with slaves. Now that Onesimus was in the household, it became his problem. And Onesimus was the close companion of young Julius. The chance rumor from Hermes aroused Hector's suspicions. He began to observe the two boys more closely. He saw nothing out of the way. He dared not approach Archippus with his questions. But Hermes would not allow the report to be shelved.

"Have you checked on Onesimus?"

"I've been watching the two of them. Nothing seems out of line."

"Well, keep on watching. I sure wouldn't trust him with my nine-year-old boy."

Onesimus knew nothing of this plot, nor did Archippus. Such rumors might have been destructive, but mercifully they remained with Hermes and Hector.

On occasion Julius became a bit unruly. He tried the patience of Onesimus, who disliked disciplining the youngster—though he had the right to do so. In the month of May, spring was at its height. Onesimus had been a slave for six months. Julius began to feel his oats. He may have had spring fever. He refused to study. Onesimus was patient and encouraging, however. When he witnessed the schoolmaster hit the boy with a mild lick he grinned to himself. Julius was humiliated—his father was Archippus. He did not report the incident to his father, but Archippus learned of it and talked with Onesimus.

"Make him toe the line. He's your responsibility. Make a man out of him."

Julius was more willing to listen to the promptings of Onesimus for a few days. They were becoming good friends. Questions, questions, questions . . .

"Why are you a slave? Are the gods for real? Why must I read Plato? Don't you think my father is too hard on me? Do you like Claudia?"

Not all of the boy's questions had easy answers. Onesimus had been reluctant to discuss his days as a free person. The nine-year-old could hardly understand his longings for freedom and family. Over the months Onesimus shared his story.

The question about the gods left him cold. His father had not been especially religious. Neither was he. Neither, for that matter, was Archippus. The stories of

Mount Olympus and its pantheon, of Ephesus and its worship, of Rome and its emperors—all of these were a part of the region's culture.

And if the gods were a part of the culture, so were Plato and many other Greek literary giants. Another part of the culture was the relationship to Rome.

Asia was a senatorial province and took pride in its orderliness. Archippus himself was a Roman citizen. His father before him had distinguished himself as a soldier and had been settled in Laodicea as a part of Rome's peace-keeping technique. Although not militaristic in his behavior, Archippus respected the legions and something of Rome's authoritarianism infected his home life.

The question about Claudia was more disturbing. Almost daily she and Onesimus met in the eating area. Julius observed their growing friendship. Personal attention seemed to characterize her serving Onesimus. Julius, as the favorite son, came in for his share. Oatmeal cakes with a touch of honey—that was his favorite snack. While he was eating, Onesimus and Claudia talked. How could a nine-year-old imagine marriage between two older friends?

Onesimus was attracted to Claudia, but the thought of marriage took a much lower priority than freedom. First things first: he must find a way to freedom. Should he mention it to Archippus? The question disturbed him. What would Archippus think? What would he say?

When the subject came up—at the initiative of Onesimus—the subject was closed—at the termination of Archippus.

"No—absolutely not. You belong to me. I purchased you. You will serve me. You will act responsibly toward Julius. If I must, I will direct Hector to keep you busy. Or . . . I will send you back to the stables and Hermes."

The mere mention of freedom seemed to change the relationship between master and slave. This was the beginning of a new harshness. There was no question about it: Archippus was master and Onesimus was slave. Julius sensed the new relationship but, caught in between, did not dare broach the subject to his father or his friend. What could he say to Archippus? What could he say to Onesimus?

The legal authorities protected the master-slave relationship—that is, they protected the master. Little sympathy was wasted on the slave. Lictors or soldiers quickly settled an occasional outbreak of slaves in a near riot. Archippus would not hesitate to put down an uprising. Onesimus did not have enough friends and allies to undertake rebellion.

3

Julius came to idolize Onesimus. If Onesimus encouraged him to study, he studied. If Onesimus suggested an outing down by the river—a fishing expedition, for example—Julius became enthusiastic. In the heat of summer, when the humidity in the river valley was unbearable, Onesimus began to talk about a mountain trip.

Most of his experience with mountains was in the hill country of Galatia, near Lystra. Yet he managed to sound like a pro.

"We could climb the slopes of Kadmos."

Both of them heard and were attracted by the possibility. Onesimus had never been an outdoorsman. He had pushed to the remote corners of his memory his terror when confronted by a snake. Stinging insects bothered him greatly. He wearied after a few miles' stroll. He much preferred the comforts of his own bed and the appetizing treats prepared by Poppae and served by Claudia.

Yet the enthusiasm of Julius encouraged him to the point of making rash plans. They need not tell Archippus or anyone else where they were going. After all, Onesimus was responsible and would act responsibly—freely, but responsibly. He and Julius made their plans.

Early on a summer morning when the sun was still a mere suggestion, the two set out. Each carried a leather bottle of water and a knapsack filled with goodies—oatmeal cookies, slices of roast lamb, firmly textured bread rolls, and fruit. Each took a staff, having seen other travelers with such. Their sandals seemed sufficient for the hike. Their scarcity of clothes caused them to shiver a bit as they made their way silently southward.

They looked upward toward the peak as they began to walk. The rocks were smooth enough, but some pebbles caused discomfort through their sandal soles. Soon the house was out of sight. Julius felt adventurous. So, for that matter, did Onesimus, though more restrained. Julius ran on ahead, and Onesimus had some difficulty keeping him in line.

After an hour the younger hiker was thirsty. He gulped at the leather bottle. Then he was hungry. He plunged into his knapsack. Onesimus was a bit more conservative with his food and drink. Another hour passed. The sun was fully visible and its heat beginning to be bothersome. Yet the road barely inclined and Kadmos seemed no nearer than when the boys set out from home.

By mid-morning the road had become a path and Laodicea receded far in the distance. The climb was wearisome.

"Let's stop for a break, Onesimus."

"Alright, but only a brief one."

The travelers consumed more water and downed more food. This time they did not begin to walk so eagerly. Their pace had slowed even before the climb began.

Suddenly a lizard ran from behind a rock. Onesimus immediately remembered a snake of long ago. He stopped and then stepped more gingerly. Julius was excited and began to hurry ahead. Then they felt a storm coming—before they were even conscious of the darkening sky. An aura of uneasiness pressed upon them before the lightning appeared in the distance. After a few seconds they heard the rumble of thunder.

Soon the lightning flashes were more frequent and the thunder clapped sharply. The appearance of both almost at the same time elicited a shout from Julius.

"Wow, that was a close one!"

Another flash and another explosion brought a response from Onesimus.

"Too close for comfort."

The boys imagined a ball of fire playing around. The rain was cool and refreshing—at first. They made for the nearest big tree and then remembered that their refuge might attract the lightning. A look around revealed a hole in the side of the rock wall. It might be a cave. They ran through the rain, now becoming increasingly wet and chilly. The hole was large enough for both of them. At least they could stay dry—but they were a long way from home and the mountain yet loomed ahead.

Meanwhile, back at the house no one knew where Onesimus and Julius were. No one had seen them leave. No one had heard them go. Claudia was the first to miss them.

"I haven't seen the two boys this morning. By this time they have been in for a snack—and it's almost time for the midday meal."

She spoke to herself as much as to anyone, then Poppae joined in the conversation.

"I thought they might have come when I was out. A batch of oatmeal cookies has been eaten, and several slices of the lamb I roasted yesterday are missing. I don't mean I counted the slices; I just mean the stack of slices is smaller than last night. You don't suppose Onesimus and Julius took them?"

By mid-morning the tutor was looking for Onesimus. Julius and Onesimus had not shown up for the morning's mathematics lesson. That brought the news to Hector and he, feeling responsible, shared the news with Archippus—shortly before the master was to make his way to a friend's house south of town. A search of the house and grounds revealed no clue—and no boys.

The search widened to other houses, but no one had seen them. No animals had been disturbed. No clothes were missing. Archippus thought it possible that Onesimus had escaped, but what about Julius? Soon a large area was alerted. Had the boys met foul play? Could they have been kidnapped or robbed or beaten?

One early riser a mile or so southward had caught a glimpse of a couple travelers early that morning, about sunrise. They appeared to be in no hurry, he said—walking leisurely on the road. They had no beast of burden. Could the boys have left so early?

The rain continued in a hard downpour on the mountainside. Onesimus now sought to protect Julius from the wind and cold rain. By this time they had almost emptied their bottles of water and their knapsacks were much lighter. They were chilled to the bone. The clouds covered the sun, and a heavy darkness covered everything else. The boys had some regrets. Now it seemed unlikely that they could climb the mountain. Indeed, they questioned when they could return home.

After midday the rain slackened. Onesimus, clearly worried, suggested that they make their way downward and homeward. Julius was almost as enthusiastic as when they left home.

"Yes, let's go home."

Both were wet and cold and weary as they picked their way carefully over the muddy, almost hidden path. The exposed rocks were slippery, causing the boys to lose their footing several times. Slowly rising, they were now bruised and sore. The vines and bushes were dripping wet, offering few handholds. Onesimus was skittish about every movement on the path but saw only a few lizards scurrying along. He sighed in relief as the path widened and eventually, hours later, ran into the road.

Bedraggled, hungry, and thirsty—the boys were glad to see the outskirts of Laodicea. They recognized the Herophilian School of Medicine. At least they could see the place where the skilled eye doctors taught and practiced. Several flocks of black sheep were grazing in the yet somewhat cloudy area.

By this time members of the household of Archippus had reached the south city limits. Justus, a kitchen slave, saw the boys first.

"There they come—down the road from Kadmos. You don't suppose they've been mountain climbing in this weather?"

The fact that they had left home in more enjoyable weather didn't occur to him. Everyone seemed glad to see Julius and to shun Onesimus. He was responsible and deserved the punishment he was sure to get.

Soon word reached Archippus, searching in a different sector of the town, and he hurried to meet his son—and his slave. He embraced Julius and began to fire questions at Onesimus.

"Where have you been? Where were you going? Why didn't you leave a message?"

When the questions received no immediate answer—they were spoken so quickly as to allow no reply—accusations poured out.

"What do you mean, exposing my son to this weather? What right did you have? You'll pay for this! Julius, come with me: I have some words for you. Onesimus, go back to the house and to your quarters. I'll deal with you later."

Saddened, if not humiliated, Onesimus joined the other slaves as they walked homeward. At the door to the kitchen stood Poppae and Claudia, glad to see Onesimus safe but worried about the punishment he would surely suffer. Onesimus went to his cot and fell across it. The day, now almost gone, had been a disappointment—and it had begun with such fun.

Hector first called on him.

"You know you're in trouble. The master is quite put out with you. To attempt escape is one thing, but to take young Julius with you is another."

"Don't you see that we were only going on an outing? Sure, we missed his mathematics class this morning. But the kid needs to get away sometimes."

"Well, the master has summoned you for the first thing in the morning. You endangered Julius, and you'll be punished."

And so Onesimus, tired and anxious, dropped off into a fitful sleep. Julius had been moved to a room nearer his father. Onesimus awoke frequently, imagining the cruel punishment awaiting him—imprisonment, lashing, consignment to the stables and Hermes.

The kitchen and eating area were strangely silent the next morning when Onesimus stopped by for warm tea and toast. It was almost as if someone in the group had died. Onesimus himself merely muttered greetings as he was forced to do. No one asked questions. He remained only for a short time.

He walked directly to the room where Archippus conducted household business. He did not see Julius, but Julius saw him, dejected and droopy.

Onesimus tapped lightly on the door and was greeted with a strong voice encouraging him to enter. The master was seated; the slave stood before him.

"You know that you not only caused great anxiety to me and to all of us, but more importantly you endangered my son's life. I have not decided on your punishment. Perhaps you have a word to speak for yourself."

"Sir, we went out on a lark. We had thought to climb Kadmos and catch a midday view of the city, the valley, and the river. We should have asked your permission. We should have told the schoolmaster. The day was beautiful before sunrise. There were no clouds in the sky. As we neared the end of the road and the beginning of the path, the clouds began to gather. When it rained we ran for cover. We were returning when the others saw us. I was not trying to escape."

"Yes, yes—so Julius told me. He defended you. He told of the trees and the lightning and finally the cave. You were right to seek refuge away from the trees. Indeed, Julius insisted that it was all his fault—that he suggested the mountain climb."

Onesimus protested with a glance at Archippus, who continued.

"I had thought you would be a good influence on the boy, and perhaps you have, but yesterday's escapade was serious. It is possible that I overestimated your maturity and entrusted you with too much responsibility. This must not happen again. You are in a favored position, and I must consider the concept of authority in the household. Yet Julius responds so well to your direction and to your friendship . . . I'll tell you what. We'll let this pass, grateful that neither of you was injured. The worst that two young men may get is a bad cold. Resume your position—but be careful that it does not occur again."

Abruptly dismissed, Onesimus heaved a sigh of relief and returned to his room near Julius. By this time Julius had returned. The boys made for the kitchen. Neither had felt like eating much in the early morning. Perhaps food would help them to forget the previous day's adventure.

Onesimus continued hearing the words in his head: "Be careful that it does not occur again."

Neither Claudia nor Poppae dared offer much sympathy. Yet their eyes spoke loudly. Poppae finally muttered a few words, followed by Claudia.

"We're glad you're back safely."

"When you turned up missing, the whole household was upset."

4

The summer days were hot and humid. An occasional afternoon's walk to the side of the river broke the monotony. To avoid the ire of his master and others, Onesimus was careful to share his plans—for the most part. But there was the time when Julius suggested a ride in late summer. Not wanting to confront Hermes or ask anyone's permission, the two boys waited until only the horses were present. They took two of their favorite mounts. No one would have objected, but they might have asked questions. Neither boy wanted to answer questions about their plans.

Onesimus and Julius rode off in silence, except for the rhythmic beating of the hoofs. The temple of Zeus at Attuda, some 13 miles west, attracted them. The tutor had talked about it and about Zeus, without the passion of belief. The dusty, hot ride ended in an oasis of growth—trees and shrubs—near the shrine. The boys walked around the structure, marveling at its huge columns, struck by its beauty. When a priest approached they turned away, not wanting their privacy invaded by some religious discussion. When a procession approached the temple, they guided their horses off the road and watched curiously the religious practices.

By afternoon they were ready for the return ride, completing it without mishap. When they approached the stables, however, Hermes met them, enraged.

"You stole a horse, Onesimus. You encouraged the master's son to accompany you. I'll report this to the master."

Somewhat wary of a fierce argument, Onesimus spoke softly.

"I didn't think you would mind young Julius riding one of his father's horses—and I knew that his father would want me to go along."

As luck would have it, no rebuke was forthcoming from Archippus. Hermes held his tongue and nurtured his resentment.

Of greater consequence was an outing on which Onesimus took Claudia. They went with the permission of Poppae, though not bothering to tell Hector—and certainly not Hermes. Onesimus fretted at the rules of the household and refused to be subject to minute details of administrative authority. With cookies and fruit, they set out for the cool shade near the river.

Onesimus was in his 16th year and Claudia in her 15th. Neither had been out alone with a girl or boy. Most of the time Onesimus spent with Julius. Most of the time Claudia spent with Poppae or another of the kitchen maids. Yet they had been friends from the first appearance of Onesimus in the kitchen. Julius had perhaps seen more clearly than anyone that the friendship was ripening.

Onesimus and Claudia talked of their friends and of their servitude. Onesimus was more interested in freedom than Claudia: she did not remember when she had not been a slave. Her mother had belonged to Archippus before her sickness and death. Her father had been killed in a slave riot—before Claudia could remember. Onesimus yet remembered his years of freedom and never gave up the hope that he would regain it.

Both found Archippus to be fair but somewhat stern. Both respected his authority, but neither liked being subject to Hector. Yet Hector was more considerate than Hermes, and the house was more comfortable than the stables.

Then they talked about themselves. Onesimus had shared his experience with only a select few in the household. He spoke frankly with Claudia.

"I want to be free, Claudia. I choke up when someone orders me around. I resent even the most reasonable suggestion from someone in authority. Sometimes only young Julius stands between me and an explosion. I love him like a brother, but I hate Archippus and Hector and Hermes and all the rest."

Claudia did not understand.

"Do you not feel free here? No one is ordering you around. Look at the sky. Look at the trees. Look at the river."

By this time they had reached the plateau from which the river was clearly visible.

"What more could you want? You have a comfortable home. You have plenty to eat."

Onesimus realized that Claudia didn't understand, and probably couldn't. So, they talked about how kind Poppae was and how Julius was growing into young manhood—in his 10th year! Then . . .

"I enjoy being with you, Claudia."

"And I enjoy being with you."

No more endearing words were spoken; they simply sat on the river's bank and tossed pebbles into the moving stream.

"Life's like that: always moving, always changing."

Claudia let her friend's comment pass. Suddenly the silence, except for the gentle movement of the water, proved oppressive. Onesimus remembered for a moment the storm's approach on the slopes of Kadmos. He and Julius had felt it before they saw it. Now, no clouds marred the sky's blue. At first there was a tremor, a slight movement. The security that was the earth beneath them was less stable. Another tremor, more severe than the first, followed quickly. Then a harsh movement of the earth itself shook them, and they knew that another earthquake had disturbed the Lycus River Valley.

Damage at the water's edge was slight. A few boulders had been dislodged and moved about. Their first thoughts were of the house in Laodicea—it was home even to Onesimus. They arose and began to walk/run eastward. A threatening crevice lay ahead, having split the path for some distance. They walked around it and beyond it. Some of the houses, mere piles of stones beforehand, now were rearranged. Their owners inspected the damage. There did not seem to be any human damage. The villa of Archippus lay just ahead. It had been badly shaken. Slaves and freed men and women were struggling to salvage a wall here or a piece of furniture there.

"Where have you two been? When there's trouble around, Onesimus, you are not around."

"We walked out to the river and returned as soon as we felt the quake."

"And we weren't doing anything out of line," Claudia protested.

The stone structure was sound. Most of the damage was on the surface.

"The gods were gentle today," Poppae spoke. "Next time they may be more severe."

"Well, if the gods had anything to do with it, they must be protesting the atheism of the Jews. They are sending an offering to Jerusalem—on the other side of the world."

Onesimus did not remember any previous mention of the Jews in the household. He knew they existed and had heard reports in Lystra of their religion. But he was not interested in religion—theirs or anyone else's. So, the charge of their atheism left him cold. Of more immediate concern was the inevitable reporting of his brief outing with Claudia.

By this time Archippus had joined the conversation.

"We did not know where you were, Onesimus. To be sure, Julius was not with you but Hector had no information. Did you tell anyone where you were going?"

The young man spoke civilly and respectfully, but not affectionately.

"We told Poppae that we were going to the river."

"When you leave this place, you are to have permission. Do you understand that?"

"Yes sir."

After a couple of hours all appeared to be sound again, in spite of the aftershocks. The inhabitants of the estate had experienced more severe shakings but had survived. Meanwhile, Archippus wondered how Onesimus would try his patience again. The earthquake had dulled his anxiety and impatience.

An earthquake can so shake the foundations as to drive men and women to examine their religious roots—of which Onesimus had none as far as he knew. Some of the other slaves had heard of a visiting teacher, neither Jew nor representing Zeus—nor even Artemis. He was talking with Laodiceans in the lecture hall of one Alexander, a local teacher and philosopher. Alexander lectured in the mornings, and Epaphras was allowed to use the hall in the afternoons. It wasn't a good time of day because most Laodiceans of means rested in the afternoon. Slaves might have more free time.

One afternoon a group of slaves, belonging to Archippus and his neighbors, secured permission to go hear Epaphras. It was a lark—in anticipation. Julius wanted to go along, but his father did not think it wise. Onesimus joined the crowd. Epaphras spoke about freedom. It was an interesting subject.

"You *can* be free . . . you *will* be free."

That sounded good!

Epaphras continued to speak, followed by a question from one of his listeners.

"God made you for freedom."

"Then what kind of god allows our masters to enslave us?"

"Freedom of the mind . . . of the heart . . . of the soul . . . is more real than freedom of the body."

Onesimus was primarily concerned with freedom of the body and said as much. He had heard that Epictetus, a neighboring slave, had taught in this manner.

"Do you know Epictetus?"

Epaphras did not know him but was interested in his teaching.

The discussion was long and involved. Once Epaphras mentioned his teacher, Paul, who lived and taught in Ephesus. He had encouraged Epaphras to come to Laodicea. Onesimus wondered if it was the same Jewish teacher by that name who had come to Lystra . . . but Epaphras was not a Jew. So, he questioned Epaphras.

"I heard of a teacher named Paul when I was a boy at Lystra. He seemed to be religious, and some of the folks there tried to worship him as a god. When he wouldn't allow it, they got mad and beat him up. Is that the same fellow who is in Ephesus?"

With his affirmative reply that it was the same Paul, Epaphras began to talk with Onesimus about his life in Lystra. He learned of the family's tragedy and the young man's enslavement. He made a mental note: Onesimus . . . that means "profitable."

The teaching session concluded for the day, and Onesimus returned home with his friends. Strange that they should prove to be friends, he thought. Perhaps they had more in common than he had supposed. No one of them seemed particularly interested in the interpretation of freedom they had heard. Freedom meant something else to them. "Soul" freedom . . . "heart" freedom . . . "mind" freedom . . . Was there some god who offered that?

Once, it was noised abroad, Epaphras had a friend along. He had the reputation of being a brilliant orator—from Alexandria, Egypt. Onesimus knew of the vast library in Alexandria and had hoped, in his Lystra days, to visit it at some time. The fact that Apollos hailed from Alexandria made him attractive. Onesimus talked with Julius about him. Julius wanted to meet him. Onesimus had heard about the other orators, principally Demosthenes.

The two boys asked and received permission of Archippus to go hear Apollos. He too was speaking in the hall of Alexander. The afternoon was cool, the hall crowded. Apollos had spoken several times and was establishing a reputation. He spoke brilliantly about the glory of God. God is so great, he said, that he called men to serve him. Although the word "serve" did not set well with Onesimus, he listened.

"His sovereignty is unlimited. He blesses those who worship him. Those who do not worship him will suffer everlasting punishment."

It was as if Apollos painted on the walls of the lecture hall—first the glories of God and his heaven and then the fiery pits of Hades. Onesimus was charmed by his charisma. He had wondered some months earlier if he could ever tend sheep and concluded that he could do that. Now he wondered if he could ever speak like Apollos. He was a bit hesitant.

And the wonderful promises of Apollos . . . Repent and be baptized and you will have life—wonderful, prosperous, satisfying life. He made no mention of behavior, speaking rather of a rugged prophet named John who lived some years before near Jerusalem. John had promised that the kingdom of heaven would come. His promise, coupled with the emphasis of Epaphras on freedom, really caught the fancy of Onesimus.

But all of this was in Laodicea. Onesimus learned that both Epaphras and Apollos had come from Ephesus. That's where he wanted to go—to Ephesus. How he would like to go to Ephesus!

However, he had overstayed his intention. He and Julius were both getting restless, and it was almost time for the evening meal. Enough oratory for one day!

5

Word of Archippus' proposed visit to Ephesus spread rapidly through the household. Julius, in talking with his father, learned about the plan. He soon mentioned it in a conversation with Onesimus. By this time, however, Claudia and Poppae had also discussed it. Hector and Hermes both longed to be included in the journey.

Onesimus was wildly enthusiastic. He made plans and then revised them. Finally, he decided that Julius was his strongest ally. The two young men went to the tutor and asked for books on Ephesus. Neither had been to the capital city of the province of Asia. Onesimus found those features described that would be of greatest attraction to a 10-year-old boy. The very size of the city, the huge theater, the presence of traveling magicians—all of these appealed to Julius. Onesimus spoke incessantly about the great time they might have in Ephesus. Then, as planned by his older friend, Julius approached his father.

"I know that you are planning a business trip to Ephasus. I have never been, and I am 10 years old. I would like to go. Perhaps you would allow Onesimus to accompany me. Then neither of us would be any trouble to you."

Experience seemed to belie that last remark, but Archippus let it pass. His son rarely pled to accompany him on a business trip. It might be good for him to escape the drudgery of the household. But Onesimus?

"I think we might arrange for you to go along, but I'm not sure about the slave."

"Father, you know what excellent care he has provided. I have advanced quickly in my philosophy and mathematics in the year he has helped me. We could talk about both of those subjects on the journey to and from Ephesus. And Ephesus itself would be an education."

Archippus agreed that a visit to Ephesus would be a learning process, though uncertain about the lessons to be learned.

For all of this time Onesimus had nothing to say to Archippus about the planned visit. But he talked frequently to Julius about his hopes—and Julius shared these hopes. As the date of departure neared, Archippus decided to include Onesimus. He called him into his administrative room.

"Onesimus, you know that I have planned a business trip to Ephesus."

"Yes, sir. Julius has told me about it."

"I have decided to take Julius along and want you to accompany him. You will be responsible for his safety—responsible to me, that is. I want no foolishness—no escape schemes, no rash plans on the part of you two. Ephesus is a large city and filled with dangerous people. Can you handle it?"

"Sir, if you will entrust me with young Julius in Ephesus, I will act responsibly."

What he did not say was that he and Julius had already planned activities in the capital city. So, it was agreed: Onesimus and Julius would go to Ephesus. Hector and Hermes would be left in Laodicea to manage the household. The tutor would also be left at the villa, enjoying a well-deserved rest from Julius—and Onesimus.

Several members of the slave and freed force were assigned special tasks. Hugies would drive the chariot's horses. Eleutherios, a freed man, would handle baggage. He and one other, Marcus, would ride the two spare horses.

The group made their way northward and traveled the high road toward Ephesus. The first night they stayed at an inn beside the road. Accommodations were somewhat primitive in contrast to the villa in Laodicea. Neither Onesimus nor Julius enjoyed the food: roast lamb (burned lamb!) and an assortment of cooked greens. For dessert they depended on the cookies Claudia and Poppae had packed.

The excitement of the morning changed to weariness by evening. Onesimus was staying with Marcus, and Julius with his father.

Marcus, a newcomer to the household, asked Onesimus about Archippus.

"He's fair, I suppose, but firm. I've been in a couple of scrapes and he's fussed and fumed, but he brought me along on this journey."

Onesimus gave Archippus the benefit of any doubts he might have had.

Early the next morning the travelers boarded the chariot and mounted the horses. The day was hot and humid, promising to become almost unbearable as they neared Ephesus, itself a river city and a seaport. Ephesus appeared to spread out all over the province. Its population was large, much larger than any city Onesimus had seen. His thoughts turned to freedom. Could he violate his master's trust on this journey?

The group approached the city from the east. From one of the vantage points they looked down on the central city, with a large and imposing temple situated near the center. The most noticeable structure lay to the west.

The theater in Ephesus was beautiful and large. It resembled a huge amphitheater, with seats made of gleaming white marble. According to reports, the seating capacity exceeded 25,000. The orchestra pit and stage could be distinguished from a distance. A broad straight road went westward toward the sea.

The little caravan paused at the scenic view but soon moved on toward their objective of finding an inn in the eastern area of the city.

"Hey, this is first class."

Onesimus talked with Julius, who was to stay in the room with him while in Ephesus. They found the beds more comfortable than the cots of the night before. A window with bars opened to the west, allowing them to look on to the center of town. Food was a first thought, this too an improvement. Fruit, dates, and figs helped to make the inevitable lamb and hard rolls palatable. Sweet cakes, wine, and goat's milk completed the menu. Onesimus chose a weakened wine. Julius chose the milk. Both boys were satisfied, weary, and sleepy.

Julius was up before daybreak. Indeed, Onesimus wondered if he had slept at all. Both were excited and began to talk about their first day's plans.

"Let's go to the theater first. Perhaps something will be happening there. We could spend the day going and looking and returning."

Onesimus agreed with Julius that the theater would be their first stop.

The two began walking from the inn shortly after sunrise, aware of the city's broad expanse. Archippus had warned them about the dangers of big city life, so they were wary of the crowds that thronged the streets.

"Coins, coins! Coins for the poor," a beggar called out.

The boys managed to bypass him. As they did, Onesimus felt an unnecessary pressure at his side and realized the man was attempting to steal his purse. He pulled away quickly and reached out to shove the would-be robber aside. Julius, sensitive to the situation, tripped him up—and the two boys ran through the crowds, their money and lives intact.

"That was a close one," Onesimus somewhat breathlessly spoke.

"We make a good team. You hit them high, and I hit them low."

Julius felt pretty confident after his assistance. He and Onesimus then noted a crowd gathered at the corner and joined it, curious as to its interest. There they saw a magician. He wasn't highly skilled—they could see his tricks, but the "oohs" and "aahs" of the crowd justified their stopping. When he asked for a coin to make it disappear, they were too sharp, too sophisticated, for that come-on.

They continued to walk, brushing against all sorts of people—young, old, slave, free, Asian, Roman, even some whom they thought to be Jews. Nothing appeared to be happening at the theater in midday. They walked around the huge structure—up and down the aisles, trying out the seats. No one seemed to care that they were there. Naturally they approached the stage and stood there looking out over the vast imagined audience. Julius could not contain himself.

"Beloved Pan and all ye other gods who haunt this place, give me beauty in the inward soul. May I have such a quantity of gold as none can carry."

Onesimus intoned a reply from another Platonic reading.

"You are young, my son, and, as the years go by, time will change and even reverse many of your present opinions."

Even out of their context, the words of Plato seemed fitting for the stage and its nonexistent audience.

The boys began their long walk across town, through the crowds, back to the inn where they were staying. Again, a crowd provoked their curiosity. This time, as they closed in, they were aware of a huge bonfire. It was a scroll-burning. Scroll after scroll was added to the flames, amounting to the hundreds. The boys had never thought about scrolls as fuel, though they had experienced some that they thought deserved no better fate. In conversation they discovered these were copies of secret incantations, magical formulas, and herbal recipes. Perhaps this is where all the really good magicians were.

"But why are they burning the scrolls? Are they no longer effective? What will become of the magicians? Who will pronounce a spell or a curse?"

Onesimus aimed his questions at no one in particular, and his answers were not to the point. Then Julius joined in the questioning.

"It's the teacher Paul. He has said that magic is wrong and wasteful of time and money. The Jew is destroying our way of life. Why, this waste represents a fortune!"

"Is he so powerful as to force this destruction?"

"No one is forced to burn his magic books. These belong to those who have been converted to this new Jewish religion. It makes folks do strange things."

After watching the flames for some time, Onesimus and Julius again began their walk toward the inn.

"Was this the same Paul of whom he had heard in Lystra, of whom Epaphras had spoken some months before in Laodicea? I'd like to hear him for myself."

Onesimus remembered that Epaphras had talked about freedom when he mentioned Paul. Onesimus was interested in that subject. Julius was less contemplative. He peered into the shops with their offerings of food, clothing, and knick-knacks but did not suggest they purchase anything.

As they walked along through mid-afternoon, a group of formerly well-dressed men ran toward them. Their clothes had been freshly torn, and they bore the marks of a beating. Their arms and faces were bloodied, and they appeared to be running for their lives. The two young men stepped aside and let them pass. Then they were amazed to see that only one man was in pursuit, swinging a club in a mad frenzy and shouting as he ran after the seven battered men.

"Jesus I know, and I know about Paul, but who do you think you are?"

"What's that all about?" Onesimus asked another by-stander.

The boys pieced the story together from several reports. They knew that some folks appeared to have evil spirits that made them act crazy. They had seen a few in Laodicea. They knew that some doctors appeared to help them. Now they learned that the men who fled were Jews, the sons of a priest, and had attempted to exorcise the man's demons with some sort of magical formula.

"Come out of him, we command you in the name of Jesus whom Paul preaches."

The formula had certainly not worked—and the would-be healers had barely escaped with their lives.

There was the name of Paul again. Even Julius became curious.

"Who is this Paul? If he's here in Ephesus, maybe we can see him. I'd like to see him cast out an evil spirit or do some other magic trick."

This was the sort of excitement that appealed to a 10-year old—as well as his older companion. By this time the inn lay ahead and the sun was beginning to set. Both boys resolved to tell Archippus of the day's events. But first—food! The menu was monotonous, but they were hungry and excited.

In excitement, Julius almost shouted as he shared with this father the events of his day.

"We saw a magician, but he wasn't very good—Onesimus and I knew his tricks. And we visited the huge theater and spoke from the stage. That was fun. And we almost got robbed, but we outwitted the robber. On the way home we saw a huge book-burning—magic formulas, we think. Paul had encouraged it. But, most exciting. . . You tell him, Onesimus. I'm out of breath."

Archippus smiled at his son's enthusiasm and barely concealed it as he turned to his slave.

"Yes, tell me about this exciting event."

"Well, sir, we were walking back here when we were met by seven men, fleeing for their lives, beaten and bloody—and they were running from one crazy man. We learned that they had tried to cast out the man's demon and couldn't. We also learned that they had used an exorcism saying about Paul and Jesus. That was the second time this afternoon Paul had been mentioned. It was an exciting day."

"It was certainly more exciting than my day. The price of sheep has gone down so sharply that I neither bought nor sold. The market is too unstable. So, tomorrow I may follow along with you."

This did not appeal to Onesimus, although he felt vindicated in arranging such an active outing—as it turned out to be.

Both boys slept soundly and awoke early. At the morning meal Archippus shared a bit of information. He had learned that Paul was indeed in town and was lecturing in the Hall of Tyrannus each afternoon. Tyrannus taught in the morning—certainly a choice hour. When the heat and humidity made listening in an enclosed hall a chore, Paul was allowed its use.

"I would like to hear him. Could I interest you two excitables to go along? You seem to stir things up."

Later, in reviewing the day's events, Onesimus realized that he would not have been so enthusiastic had he known that Paul was a traveling preacher. To be sure, traveling teachers occasionally talked about the gods but usually in a condescending, if not degrading, frame of reference. His own father was not a traveling teacher but had very little to say about religion. But Onesimus did not know much about Paul. Neither did Archippus.

Between the inn and the Hall of Tyrannus stood the Temple of Artemis. The area was something of a spawning ground for new ideas, strange faiths, and wild forms of religion. The cult of Isis had been transported from Egypt and had many worshipers. And there were always the Jews. In and out of their synagogue they professed a loyalty to their temple in Jerusalem, even sending gifts to it regularly from Ephesus and Colossae and Laodicea—and perhaps from all over the world. The asiarchs, civil officials charged with patriotism and loyalty to the Roman Empire, encouraged emperor worship.

But Artemis was the goddess of the Ephesians. Some distance from the temple, shops lined both sides of the road. Most of them offered replicas of the temple made of terra cotta, marble, or silver. Many represented the goddess herself, sitting in a niche with her lions beside her. These were sold to worshipers and offered as gifts to the goddess. Archippus began to talk about the uselessness of such activities.

"You know that the cold stone image can't use the gifts. They go to the priests who in turn sell them or, in the case of silver, melt them down. And the poor people, who spend their hard-earned coins, are not helped one iota by the sacrifice. Taking advantage of the poor like that makes my blood boil."

"Are not all religions like that, sir?" asked Onesimus, finding something in common with his master.

Julius then joined the conversation—before being cut short by his father.

"I've heard and read about this temple. There are dances and wild women and priests and priestesses . . ."

"And some of those activities you will not witness!"

They did not enter the temple. Reports had it that the image at its center was carved with multiple breasts, emphasizing the nature of the fertility cult. The image was believed by some to have fallen intact from heaven. Onesimus snorted at that bit of conversation. The approach to the temple from the other side was equally busy with Artemis business.

A short distance beyond the temple the three travelers saw a crowd gathered outside the Jewish synagogue. Thinking that it must be a day of worship, they moved to the other side of the road. As they drew nearer, they realized that an argument was in progress.

"Ah, you could not stand the heat of synagogue truth, so you have moved next door. You have shown your colors. You are no longer a Jew. You have forsaken Abraham. God will forsake you."

The speaker was clearly a synagogue teacher. The object of his wrath was a smaller man, plainly dressed, yet recognizably Jewish. He appeared to be somewhat bow-legged and had sharp features and accosting eyes.

"I am an apostle to the Gentiles. You Jews had your chance at the Good News. You rejected it when I offered it to you. You forced me out of the synagogue. Fortunately, some of my countrymen have joined me in the Hall of Tyrannus. Perhaps its convenience to others will be attractive."

It was then that Archippus and the two boys saw the Hall of Tyrannus adjacent to the synagogue.

"That took a lot of nerve—setting up shop next door," observed Onesimus.

By this time Paul had entered the hall, and many followed him. Archippus, Onesimus, and Julius stood near the rear. Fiery, independent, committed—those words characterized Paul. He spoke of the season.

"Artemisia draws near, and many Ephesians will prostrate themselves before the cold, lifeless image. Artemis has never lived. The goddess is nonexistent. My master lived and was crucified. This is the day my master died."

Onesimus could not restrain the thought in his head: *Would that I could say that about my master!*

Yet Archippus had been kind on the journey, and the affection between Onesimus and Julius was genuine. Once again, the slave heard the word "freedom" and listened intently.

"For freedom Christ set you free. Live like it. Treasure your freedom. Use your freedom."

"Fine words from one who never knew slavery!" Onesimus mumbled

"What did you say?" Julius responded.

"I was simply talking to myself."

During the long discourse Archippus listened intently. The two boys were restless but remained in the hall. After a couple of hours Paul allowed questions from those gathered before him. Clearly many sympathized with his position. Some opposed him. A lively discussion proceeded.

The crowd was reluctant to leave. Onesimus recognized Epaphras with Paul. There was a younger man—alert, friendly. He heard him introduced as Timothy. Apparently Paul had a sizable group of friends and supporters. Archippus met a doctor, Luke, and was impressed by his intelligence and culture. Not many boys the age of Julius were present. Julius and Onesimus stood together. Archippus was interested, which surprised the boys. He had rarely heard a religious theme with any show of interest. Then he spoke with one of Paul's associates.

"Epaphras, I understand that you were in Laodicea some months ago. I believe my slave heard you and was impressed."

"Yes, Paul arranges for us to spread out from Ephesus to share the Good News with all of the province."

"If you plan to return, we would be happy to welcome you as a guest at our house."

"I doubt if I will return to Laodicea in the near future, but I will be in Colossae for a few days in the early summer."

"I will look forward then to seeing you there. The doctrine that Paul presents intrigues me."

"Suffering love has proved to be the most powerful force in all the world. As innocent as the theme sounds, Paul has stirred up a good bit of hostility—from the Jewish leaders next door as well as the worshipers of Artemis."

With this final statement, Epaphras moved to talk about Paul and his Good News in other groups.

Archippus was strangely silent and somewhat subdued for the rest of the day. Because business affairs were not proving profitable, he planned to return with his group to Laodicea on the next day. Onesimus and Julius thought of many sights they'd like to see, so were disappointed at the change in plans. Yet they would have a great deal to talk about on their return journey and to tell the household when they arrived at the villa . . . the theater, the magician, the book-burning, the demoniac, the temple, the synagogue, the Hall of Tyrannus, Paul and Timothy and Epaphras and Luke. They slept soundly at the inn.

6

The journey back from Ephesus proved uneventful. Archippus appeared to be meditating, and the boys found excitement in the scenery and occasional stops. They were the envy of the household when they returned. Claudia seemed especially charmed by the reports Onesimus brought. Julius spent more time with Poppae. He especially valued his cook/friend.

So began the second summer of Onesimus in slavery to Archippus. He was now 17, and Julius 11. Onesimus yet remembered his parents and a few friends in Lystra. He had not heard from or about any of them. Did they even know or care what had happened? He and Julius were talking about the visit to Ephesus when Julius spoke.

"Onesimus, do you remember that younger fellow with Paul. Was his name Timothy?"

"That was his name alright."

"Is he Paul's son?"

"No, I don't think so."

Then the cogs began to whirl in Onesimus' brain. It suddenly occurred to him that the Timothy he had met in Ephesus had spoken with a Lycaonian accent—so slight yet so familiar that Onesimus had not responded to it. He remembered too that something had been said about his home in Lystra. Why had he been so dull after listening to Paul for two hours? He had not even noticed the reference at the time.

Onesimus had heard his parents talk about young Timothy going off with Paul, but his mother was a Jew, so Onesimus did not know him. It was strange that Timothy should leave Lystra with Paul and Onesimus should leave Lystra with Archippus. Yet Timothy had gone willingly and with his parents' knowledge. He must see Timothy again. But where? How?

Conversation with Julius was at a lull. An invitation to go to the fruit market prompted the boy's interest. They set out, two friends—the one free, the other slave. The market, a short distance from the villa, was unattended. The boys helped themselves to some choice morsels of fruit on display. As they strolled through and away, the owner came on the scene. He yelled at the petty thieves, and they responded by breaking into a run.

Soon several people joined the chase. Shopkeepers, accustomed to working together in such cases, caught up with them. With accusations and the evidence of incriminating fruit, the boys were held for the authorities.

About that time Hector walked by. In some relief Onesimus called to him. He sized up the situation, reassured the shopkeeper whose fruit they had taken, paid dearly for it, and walked back to the villa with the boys—but with resentment in his voice.

"Onesimus, the master is going to be angry with you. You have clearly managed to get young Julius in trouble again."

Onesimus knew he was in trouble and hated for Hector to be his accuser.

"We didn't take much fruit. The owner was not there. We were going to pay for it."

"Sure, sure, tell that to Archippus."

And they did—the sordid story of the thievery. Archippus reacted as expected: angrily.

"Why did I ever call you Onesimus? You have been anything but profitable to me. I'm tempted to sell you—if I could get a good price . . ."

Julius had been dismissed to his room. Only Archippus and Onesimus were left.

"I'm sorry, sir. We should not have taken the fruit."

About that time another servant interrupted them, giving Archippus a sealed letter.

"This just came by post."

"Go to your room, Onesimus, while I decide what to do with you."

Onesimus left Archippus alone with his letter. He broke the seal and read:

> *Epaphras, minister of the Lord Jesus Christ, with Paul and Luke and Timothy to Archippus our brother-to-be, greeting. We are well and the Hall of Tyrannus is usually crowded as Paul preaches the Good News of God's redemption in Christ. We remember your interest and your friendship. I plan to be in Colossae for a few days in July. I hope to see you on the way, perhaps on the afternoon of the 15th. God be gracious to you. Epaphras.*

"That's only a few days from now. I wonder if Epaphras will be alone. He wrote nothing of companions. Very well, if I can restrain Onesimus . . . and Julius . . . I will enjoy his visit."

There was no restraining of the young men. Perhaps it was the heat and humidity. Perhaps it was the fact that the tutor was taking a brief vacation. Perhaps, and this was certainly a part of it, Onesimus was becoming increasingly restless in his role. Julius had become the younger brother he had never had, but he chafed at the fact of slavery.

There was the almost disastrous outing on the river. They latched two rotting logs together for a makeshift raft, but the raft proved un-river-worthy and they fell into the water. One of the logs struck Onesimus as he sought to insure the safety of Julius, leaving him momentarily unconscious as Julius pulled him to the bank. They rested there, thoroughly wet, until they dried in the sun. Onesimus had a knot on his forehead that he had to explain—first to Claudia and Poppae and then to Hector. Of course, the report then reached Archippus.

"At least Julius is safe, but I'm not sure how long I can put up with that teenage boy," Archippus responded—and his usual rebuke followed.

A second attempt at climbing Cadmos proved more successful. The boys, now veteran climbers, made it to the top, surveyed the scene, and then climbed down. When Julius reported triumphantly to his father, Archippus took a dim view of the unauthorized expedition, however successful, muttering to himself that something had to be done.

About this time the visit from Epaphras drew near. The honored guest from Ephesus deserved well-nigh regal treatment. All of the household was involved in sprucing up the property. On the afternoon of July 15 the lone horseman arrived. Others in the party had gone on to Colossae. The two older friends were elated.

"Epaphras, how glad I am to see you! I appreciate the time and trouble you have gone to in coming to Laodicea. Tell me, how are Paul and Timothy and the others? Paul did not come with you?"

"I wanted to see you and the two young men: Julius, I believe, is your son and Onesimus is your slave. Paul sends his greetings. He is caught up with the ministry in Ephesus but wanted to share the Good News with this area. And frankly, we are both concerned that your faith might produce a confession, a commitment to the Lord Jesus."

"I was struck by your greeting me in the letter as 'brother-to-be.' I am grateful for your confidence in me and your friendship. I have been thinking seriously about identifying with the church, though we are so far from Ephesus and the regular services Paul conducts."

"Then perhaps you will join us in Colossae for some of the meetings. Dr. Luke and Timothy came with me and are now in Colossae."

"That's great. I'll be glad to see them. I heard Paul speak of forgiveness, mercy, love, hope, redemption, fellowship, commitment, and faith. All of these concepts are attractive to me. I have experienced some resentment at the tragic death of my wife several years ago, leaving me with Julius and the responsibilities of the household."

"I did not know . . ."

"Hear me out: I may have felt some guilt as well. She was sick for many months before I sensed it, and then she wasted away. By the time we acknowledged the condition as being so serious, she was too far gone for the doctors to help. If I had been more attentive to her . . . Perhaps I have transferred some of that guilt in my overprotection of my son. And yet I have difficulty relating to him. He is so happy when with Onesimus. And I, a father figure, seem only to rebuke or chastise him."

"You are right to hear forgiveness and mercy and hope in Paul's preaching. This is why we refer to it as the Good News. So much of life is filled with guilt and cruelty and despair that this message cuts across the grain of life as we live it. I will not urge you on the basis of our friendship, but on the basis of your need. Yet I am your friend, and I would welcome you to the household of faith. God loves you, Archippus. The Lord Jesus died for you."

"I have heard the message but must have time to absorb it—to mix it up with faith. Come now. Will you stay the night?"

Already, twilight began to shroud the slopes of Cadmus.

"I will be honored to be your guest. Tomorrow morning, I—or perhaps we—will ride to Colossae. I am anxious to preach in the hall we have rented."

The evening meal was served in the dining room off the private quarters of Archippus. At the last minute Julius, feeling out of place with the two older men, persuaded his father to allow Onesimus to join them. While Archippus heard Epaphras speak of fellowship and commitment and faith, Onesimus heard only freedom. He must somehow gain that freedom . . . but not in a sermon! Suddenly a question from Epaphras interrupted the slave's musing.

"Do you remember Timothy, Onesimus?"

"Of course, I do. He's the young man from Lystra, isn't he? You see, my home was in Lystra too until . . ."

He hesitated to speak harshly of the interruption of his life—he could not blame Archippus for the death of his parents. He continued to listen to the visitor.

"Timothy and Dr. Luke are in Colossae and will join me in our mission."

"What is that 'mission'?"

Julius imagined a military mission or an educational mission or a cultural mission. He could not identify Epaphras with a fun mission, though his father's friend had been kind to him.

"That mission is to share the good news of God's love in Christ Jesus."

The phrase "God's love" evoked a negative response in the mind of Onesimus, but he restrained himself. Julius voiced his thoughts, though.

"I can remember my mother. She loved me."

He had not intended to rebuke his father, but Archippus felt the sting of the slight. Epaphras tried to cover.

"Of course, she did. And your father loves you too."

"I do, I do indeed," muttered Archippus to no one in particular.

So, it was arranged. Epaphras left early the next morning for Colossae. Archippus was to follow soon afterward. By this time Julius and Onesimus sensed the spirit of adventure. Julius secured his father's permission, and the two young men went along.

The hall in Colossae, rented for the occasion, was used, as was the Hall of Tyrannus in Ephesus, in the morning hours. After lunch Epaphras and his friends met to talk about God and his goodness. It was here that Archippus decided to become a Christian. He announced his faith and commitment to share the Good News with others. Unfortunately, Julius and Onesimus had become interested in some activity on the street at the time.

The darkening clouds began to produce rain. Julius and Onesimus had wandered some distance from the hall and knew they might be in trouble. They made a dash through the street, splashing and splashed. The rain increased in intensity; they were soaked. Dripping wet and cold, they sought to slip in the back door without being noticed. But Archippus had missed them as soon as the rain began. He voiced his concern so that almost all of those present anxiously awaited the boys' return.

The downpour and the condition of Onesimus and Julius dampened some of the enthusiasm of Archippus' commitment to the Christians. Conversation now revolved around methods of drying out and warming up. The new faith of Archippus did not immediately soften his anger at the boys. Onesimus especially was to blame.

Meanwhile Timothy talked with Onesimus, and the slave again noted the slight accent. They talked about Lystra and found some common interests. To be sure, their families had not known one another and so the boys had enjoyed no contact. Yet Timothy listened sympathetically as Onesimus poured out his tale of woe, made more difficult by his experience with the rain. He could not conceal his burning desire for freedom and his resentment at the injustice of his slavery.

It was clear as Archippus, Julius, and Onesimus traveled back to Laodicea after the rain ceased that Archippus, for all his newfound and confessed faith, was unhappy with the boys. Although they shared their spirit of adventure, Onesimus, as the older and more responsible one, was blamed for the escapade.

During the night Onesimus noticed that Julius was restless and appeared to have the sniffles. By daylight he was tossing and turning on his cot and burning with fever. Onesimus immediately shared the news of his condition with Poppae, whose skill with home remedies was well known. Poppae looked in on him—he was too sick to get up from his bed—and suggested that Archippus be told. The master/father came for a few moments and was quite concerned.

"We must have a doctor to examine Julius. I know that Colossae is several miles away, but Dr. Luke is there. I want Luke to minister to Julius. Onesimus, can I trust you to go to Colossae and bring Luke to Laodicea? I did not summon help soon enough for my wife; I must not make the same mistake with Julius. Ride, Onesimus: go to Colossae and return with Dr. Luke."

Ignoring any necessity for preparation, Onesimus, anxious about Julius and drawn by his sympathy to Archippus, went immediately to the stable, saddled his favorite horse, and rode toward Colossae. Both he and the horse were weary when they arrived at the inn where Epaphras, Timothy, and Luke were staying. He described the situation quickly and asked Luke to accompany him back to Laodicea. Epaphras and Timothy encouraged Luke to go, but he was on the way almost by the time he heard of their urging. He and Onesimus rode swiftly.

Archippus never left Julius alone. Poppae ministered to him, doing little more than placing cold compresses on his head and face, listening as only a woman can to a child's fretting. The father had never been so concerned or so attentive. Julius responded to his father's love. Where there had been neglect and resentment for it, now there was his father's presence and gratitude for it. Yet the fever remained and the youngster suffered.

Onesimus and Luke arrived between mid-morning and midday. Luke dismounted at the house, then Onesimus tended to the horses. Archippus welcomed Luke to the room where he and Poppae had sought to care for Julius. The doctor set to work examining the patient, with Poppae close in attendance. At his request for tea she moved to the kitchen and returned with some. Luke mixed it with some herbs and gave the dosage to Julius. By this time Julius was experiencing chills, so warm bed coverings were heaped on him. The hours passed by slowly.

With time to think, Onesimus realized he was on his own—as he had been on the long ride to Colossae. Why had he not fled? Why did he not escape now? Was it his love for Julius or his loyalty to Archippus? He grimaced a bit at the second possibility—certainly not loyalty to his master/owner. He thought to himself: *I won't let another chance like that pass. As soon as Julius recovers I'll make myself scarce around here.*

Julius recovered, thanks to the prayerful attention of a skilled doctor, the new devotion of his father, and the loving concern of the household. Luke returned to the mission at Colossae and helped in the establishment of a group of believers there—among them Archippus.

Among the friends of Archippus in Laodicea was Philemon who, with his wife, Apphia, was also drawn to the Good News. Like Archippus, Philemon and Apphia became a part of the group of believers in Colossae. They appeared to be the only ones in Laodicea, but the center of activity was in Colossae. In some ways Laodicea was the more important city. It was financially independent of the government. Indeed on at least one occasion it had allowed Cicero to cash his treasury bills of exchange at a local bank. But that had been a century earlier. Yet it remained a part of the local folklore.

Perhaps it was a normal development that attracted Archippus to Colossae. His livestock interests were not confined to Laodicea, nor were his business associates. When Epaphras sought to strengthen the church at Colossae with lay leadership, he recognized that Archippus would be a real asset if he only lived in Colossae. He dared mention it to Archippus, who promised to think about it. Could he make the move to a new locale and preserve the household? What changes would be necessary? He did not trust Onesimus, regardless of his son's friendship and the slave's quick trip to Colossae and his return with Dr. Luke. He supposed he would market Onesimus.

Poppae was already a slave by choice only. Though technically she was in that relationship, her freedom of movement and function was assured. She would stay with the household out of loyalty. Claudia was younger and would probably benefit from being freed. There had never been any question about her loyalty—yes, he would give her freedom. Hector and the others had a slave mentality and would feel insecure in any other relationship. That meant the proposed move to Colossae would involve two personnel changes: Onesimus was to be sold and Claudia freed. He felt that his new relationship with Julius would help to ease any dissatisfaction with the sale of Onesimus, so he proceeded with his plans.

"Onesimus, I have decided to move to Colossae so that I might share in the ministry of the young church. As I have told you before, I intend to put you on the market. I have a heavy investment in you, and I need to preserve that investment. Julius will certainly miss you, and I will too, but this is my decision."

"Sir, I know that I have disappointed you many times. I want my freedom, however, and I intend to get it—perhaps not from you, but from my new master. Slavery is unjust. I can hardly imagine your supporting it when you profess to be a follower of Jesus."

"Enough of that. You will be notified of the new arrangements. I shall expect complete submission to the law of the land."

What you expect and what you get are two different things, Onesimus muttered to himself as he bowed and left the room.

By this time he had heard of Claudia's release. A plan began to form in his mind. He intended to escape anyhow, and Claudia would be free. He had learned to like her a great deal, though he had not told her of his feelings. He was 19 years old and she only a little younger. Why could they not marry and live happily somewhere in the empire? He would broach the subject to her.

Claudia was in the dining room preparing to serve the evening meal. He approached her, indicating he would like to talk. She sat at a table and he joined her.

"Claudia, I first learned to respect you, and then to like you, and now I love you. I want you to marry me. You are free to go. We will have a happy life together."

"Onesimus, I am free to be sure, but you are yet a slave. We cannot marry."

The word "slave" proved upsetting. In an angry fit that was unlike him, he seized her arm and began to lead her forcefully out of the dining room. She protested and Poppae heard the commotion. She and Claudia together were too much for Onesimus, and he backed off and out of the room. Soon, word passed around the members of the household and eventually reached Archippus. Angrily he immediately advertised Onesimus for sale. Julius pled with his father but without result. Onesimus was to be sold.

Sulking at the immature action and Claudia's rejection, Onesimus began to plan his escape. Archippus was a considerate master and did not carefully guard his slaves, so escape would be easy. The slave realized he must leave the area. Colossae and Hierapolis would be as risky as Laodicea . . . Ephesus . . . of course. Only a few days' ride from Laodicea, and he would be lost in the crowds of the city.

So, while Archippus prepared to move his household to Colossae, Onesimus prepared to move to Ephesus. He had no money, only youthful enthusiasm. Early in the morning he slipped out of the room he shared with Julius and into the kitchen. There he quietly gathered some food, bread and fruit primarily. Then he slipped out of the house and toward the stables. The animals knew him and so were not disturbed. Onesimus led his horse out into the lot and away from the house. They walked quietly and quickly together until they were some distance down the road. Then he mounted the horse and, slapping him good-naturedly on the side, headed for Ephesus and freedom.

7

The escaping slave was alone on the road for a distance. He had not carefully planned his journey, but he had made it with Archippus and Julius on the previous occasion. He chose not to ride through Colossae and the upper road, moving more directly toward Ephesus, although the road was not so well maintained or traveled as the one from Colossae to Ephesus.

At first he rode as if on a lark. The crisp autumn air and the clear skies underscored his newfound freedom. At age 19 and in robust health, full of life and enthusiasm, Onesimus did not consider himself a law violator or a hunted fugitive. A shady spot, sometimes with a spring, attracted him while on his leisurely ride. He rationed his food and allowed his horse to graze while he rested.

On the second day he did not begin so early. The road was more heavily traveled, and the sense of being a fugitive began to dawn on him. Onesimus became painfully aware that both he and his horse belonged to someone else. *What will Archippus do to recover his property?* Now he noticed fellow travelers, eyeing him with the suspicion that guilt produces. Some waved to him, but for the most part he did not return the greeting. He began to wonder—now about Archippus, now about Julius, now about Claudia.

The household of Archippus was severely upset by the flight of Onesimus. No one was really surprised, but several were disappointed: Claudia, Poppae, and Julius. Archippus was angered and immediately sent Hector to Colossae to search for him. What more logical destination for a runaway slave? Yet Archippus restrained Hector in his charge.

"Do not treat him harshly. Bring him back here. I want him and the beast in good shape."

Archippus had determined that Onesimus had taken nothing else except a bit of food.

Julius was crushed. For almost four years Onesimus had been his constant companion. Now 13, Julius treasured close friendships. Yet he must have sensed the frustration of his friend and his longing for freedom. He secretly hoped that

Onesimus would not be caught. Sometime, somewhere, somehow, he would see his friend again. He had confidence in his friend's ability to make good his escape.

Claudia talked with Poppae about the escape. There was hardly any other topic of conversation among the servants.

"I really miss him. I did not know how much I cared for him."

"Nor I. He and Julius were always underfoot."

But Onesimus was gone, Claudia had her freedom, and Poppae enjoyed the new pittance Archippus paid her. All busily involved themselves with the move to Colossae. Even Archippus was so anxious that all would go well, he gave up the pursuit of Onesimus for the time being.

Onesimus did not know this. Every traveler proved a threat on the third day. The farther he rode from Laodicea, the more insecure he felt. His food was almost gone, and Ephesus was yet a day's journey. He had not pushed himself or his horse.

Then, as Onesimus rested in a shady grove, he heard the voice of a young man who appeared to be close to his own age and also riding a horse.

"Hello, there. Where are you going?"

"I'm going to Ephesus to find work"

Onesimus invented the reason for his flight. He had not troubled himself about his support in the city.

"That's where I'm headed too. Perhaps we can travel together. Where are you from?"

"My home is in Lystra. My parents had a little shop there. I thought I might find similar work in Ephesus."

"Yeah, there are many, many shops in Ephesus. Have you ever been there?"

By this time Onesimus felt more comfortable in the conversation.

"One time we spent several days visiting. What do you plan to do in the big city?"

"Make a pile of money! The biggest business in town is the Temple of Artemis. I'm going to learn to be a silversmith—apprentice myself to one of the old-timers and take over his trade. . . I may even take it over before he's ready! My name's Alexander. What's yours?"

"Onesimus. Let's ride together. Maybe we can find some more friends there."

"Maybe some girls . . ."

Onesimus was not quite ready to forget Claudia, despite her refusing to flee with him.

The two young men rode off together, racing a bit, then reining in. Soon other travelers stirred up more dust, and they knew Ephesus was close ahead. Alexander had not been to Ephesus before, so Onesimus led the way to temple row—shop after shop with wares either in front or just inside. There did not appear to be much business, but they stopped at one that looked more prosperous than the rest and Onesimus approached the shopkeeper in a friendly fashion.

"Need some help?"

"Well, yes, I do. My assistant has quit to take another job. Have you ever worked in a shop?"

"I worked with my parents in Lystra. I need a job—and you need someone to help."

It was almost too good to be true.

When Alexander asked about an apprenticeship, Demetrius the shopkeeper directed him to an acquaintance a few doors beyond.

Demetrius proved to be a good businessman, driving a hard bargain with Onesimus. Still, it was a job and a place to stay. After going over the inventory and checking the pricelist, Onesimus greeted his first customer.

"What can I help you with?"

Demetrius stayed in the background.

"I want a silver shrine to offer in the temple. My wife is ill, and I need to placate Artemis."

At this point Onesimus suffered a rude awakening. What would Archippus think about this turn of events—his slave selling shrines for the worship of Artemis? For that matter, what would Timothy think?

He successfully completed the sale, carefully counting out the change and placing the proceeds in the bag so designated. This pleased Demetrius.

Alexander stopped in and shared his news.

"I'm in! I'll serve as an apprentice making silver shrines. My master will feed me, clothe me, give me a place to sleep, and even pay me a weekly wage."

He was excited, and Onesimus shared his excitement.

"Will you be staying in the back of the shop down the street?"

"I will. We'll get to stay in touch with one another."

After dark, with the shops closed and the evening meal completed, the two young men sat on the street and talked well into the night. Surprisingly they learned as they trusted one another that they were both runaways—Onesimus from Laodicea and Alexander from Colossae. Both had been kept so close to their own households that they had not seen each other. Onesimus told of his visits to Colossae. Alexander had visited Laodicea on one occasion. It was their first night in Ephesus. They were excited and tired—and glad for their jobs.

Shortly before midnight they separated, Alexander walking down the street to his lodging and Onesimus to his. Both slept soundly, and Onesimus arose early. Breakfast was simple—bread and fruit—but welcome. Early in the morning Demetrius summoned him.

"I want you to open shop today. I have some business elsewhere. I trust you, though I don't know much about you."

Onesimus, eager to please, responded quickly.

"You won't be sorry. I'm honest with your receipts and with my time. I'll take care of things."

At that Demetrius left the shop.

A few customers came in, some to shop and some to buy but all to talk. The name of a Jew named Paul was on every tongue. Onesimus listened carefully as different ones spoke.

"I saw it with my own eyes. I never thought I'd see it. It was incredible."

"I was there too. I wouldn't miss a show like that in the arena. They brought this little Jew out and prepared to loose a lion on him."

"What was the charge?" asked Onesimus.

Instead of ignoring him as he half expected, they talked freely.

"You see, this fellow, Paul, has been lecturing or talking or something in the Hall of Tyrannus. Many Ephesians have heard him. He speaks of one, Christ, whom he relates as the Son to God."

"Many Ephesians have heard him and have believed too. They have become members of a group he calls the *ekklesia*, the church, or the assembly."

"And one of those who believed was the governor's wife. When Hieronymous heard about it he was enraged. He knew how important loyalty to Artemis was for the province's prosperity. He talked with others and discovered that many were hostile to Paul and his teaching."

"So, he closed his wife up in the governor's palace and placed charges against Paul—meddling, proselyting, alienation of affections."

The latter charge was the most serious. Any time home ties were publicly threatened, heads were apt to roll. The stories continued throughout the day . . . speaker after speaker . . . some interrupting . . . some muttering . . . some arguing . . . some avowing. Demetrius did not return. Onesimus could believe most of what he heard about the governor and Paul. He was interested in the outcome but found it impossible to believe.

"So, they released the lion and the animal leaped forward. All of the crowd rose to its feet, urging the kill. Paul stood still. The lion, both fast and ferocious, stopped short. Would you believe it? The lion lay down at his feet and licked him."

At this Onesimus first chuckled and then laughed aloud.

"Did you witness that? Did you see the lion lie calmly and peaceably at his feet?"

"No, I didn't see it. The crowd was standing, so I couldn't see."

"But I heard a terrible roar from the crowd, and other animals were released on Paul. Then there came this terrific dark cloud, and it began to rain and hail. The crowds were running for cover, and I looked out to see all of the animals fleeing the hall except for the lion who didn't seem to mind. Later I heard that the governor's ear was almost torn off by the huge hailstones."

Although Onesimus had said little—he mainly listened—he now interjected a comment.

"That's the most ridiculous story I've ever heard. I suppose Paul and the lion walked off the field together, bosom buddies."

The witness claimed to have seen part of the event and to have heard about the rest. Onesimus charged it off to popular superstition. He did, however, note the importance of Paul in Ephesus. He had met Paul. Perhaps he could use that relationship to his advantage. The conversion of the governor's wife was one thing, but the conversion of the lion was something entirely different!

It seemed to Onesimus that his visitors had not been sharply critical of Paul, only impressed by him. He must hear Paul again for himself, but he must be careful. Demetrius returned by mid-afternoon and heard reports of the day's business—and shop talk. He indicated that these fellows liked nothing better than a good story—and liked to stretch the truth. Onesimus agreed with him.

By the end of the first full day in the shop Onesimus had come to terms with the merchandise. After all, the chief religion of Ephesus was the worship of Artemis. Since he had not come from a fanatically religious family, he did not fully appreciate the cost of the gifts to the temple. On the other hand, if this was their thing, then let them have at it!

He remembered the friendship of Timothy, the good news of Epaphras, and the person of Paul, but Archippus had become a believer and it hadn't seemed to make any difference in his treatment of his slave. Perhaps one religion was as good or as bad as another.

The shop talk gave way to the shop's closing, the evening meal, and a visit by Alexander. His day had been rough—learning the hot, dirty, smelly basics of smithing. This perhaps prompted his suggestion that they take a walk—in the direction of the temple. Onesimus thought it sounded like a good suggestion, and they leisurely strolled along. Others were going in the same direction. Apparently, something was scheduled to happen. Then they began to pick up on conversations.

"I can be very religious when I'm with that dancer Helene," one man a bit older than Onesimus and Alexander spoke.

"You go with Helene; I'll worship with Alicia," his friend replied.

At first Onesimus and Alexander did not understand. Only when they came to the open door and saw the women did they sense that the temple priestesses were prostitutes and the so-called worship was actually a sexual exercise. The women appeared to be of various ages. The older ones were coarse in demeanor and dress. They were more aggressive, standing out in front of the temple, almost assaulting Alexander and Onesimus.

"Come on in, young men. Give yourselves in the worship of Artemis."

The two young men resisted the women's advances and then noticed a much younger girl. She could not have been more than 11 or 12. Surely, she could not belong to the temple cult. But she did and reached out to grasp the arm of Onesimus. He was overwhelmed, not only in his sexuality, but in his sympathy. Uninitiated into the looseness of city living, the young men hurried on past the temple—but not without several invitations to join in the "worship." Another day perhaps. . .

Onesimus wondered if the faith of Paul and Archippus offered similar experiences, but reasoned it probably did not. Was the worship of Artemis, then, a young man's faith? Were Paul and Archippus too old to respond?

Demetrius stayed in the shop the next day. Conversation yet revolved around Paul and the Jews and their threat to the worship of Artemis. Onesimus listened without comment and thought about how he could visit the Hall of Tyrannus one afternoon. Perhaps he could manufacture an excuse to take off from work at the shop. He thought about an extended delivery schedule, but so far Demetrius had not asked him to deliver any merchandise. He somehow felt that his employer would not look favorably on the real reason. But an opportunity came unexpectedly.

Demetrius was the leader of a group of silversmiths and shopkeepers in Ephesus. Sometimes their conversation revolved around the local religion, the worship of Artemis. At such times their religious devotion sounded sincere enough. At other times their interest was clearly less religion and more business. They worked together to promote the sale of images made from silver and other materials, images useful in making an offering to Artemis. Their common craft and their interlocking business interests drew them together in a somewhat binding relationship. When the popularity of Artemis was threatened, their profit was endangered. The presence of many Jews in Ephesus had long been a point of contention. With the coming of Paul, many native Ephesians were becoming less interested in the ardent worship of Artemis.

So, one afternoon Demetrius assigned Onesimus the task of delivering some notices to other craftsmen. The notices announced a planned meeting two evenings hence.

"I'll be here in the shop. Take the afternoon and get these in the hands of our friends. If you complete the task, take some time off."

Onesimus fully intended to do just that.

"Yes, sir. I'll get them out."

And so it happened that by mid-afternoon Onesimus approached the Hall of Tyrannus.

The hall was crowded. He slipped in at the rear of the crowded hall, thinking no one noticed and trying to get lost in the crowd. He heard Paul speaking.

"Some of you have come because of the story of the lion. Don't worry about the lion. Be concerned rather about the crowds in the stands. They urged the lion on. The lion had more sense and more compassion than did the crowds. In any event they confused Paul with Androcles. The story has been greatly exaggerated. Ask someone who was there. I'm not a lion-tamer. My name's not even Daniel. I'm not primarily concerned with why you have come; I'm just glad you have come. I will say this: God rescued me from the mouth of the lion. The method is not so important. The fact that I'm here today is extremely gratifying to me—and I hope to you."

I'm glad you're here, but I would like to know how you escaped. You certainly sound casual about it, Onesimus muttered to himself.

Then he realized that a part of his muttering had been audible. In embarrassment he became silent. Paul continued on a favorite theme.

"It is the truth that makes you free—the truth about God, the truth about yourself."

At that point Onesimus recognized the man who rose to question Paul. It was Epictetus, a slave friend from the Lycus Valley. He was interested, like Onesimus, in the subject of freedom.

"I'm a slave on a visit to Ephesus with my master. Your message is a mockery of my status. What sort of freedom do you offer me?"

Onesimus listened carefully to Paul's reply.

"Your physical bonds are uncomfortable, I am sure, but your spiritual bonds are of much greater significance. Your perception of truth and your loyalty to truth will set you free."

Epictetus leaped to his feet and shouted his true feelings.

"There are many slaves in Ephesus—as many as there are free men. What you are saying is gobbledygook. Lead us in a crusade for freedom. Away with slavery from the face of the earth!"

Onesimus squirmed uncomfortably at this cry. He had escaped and wanted no part in a slave uprising.

Paul spoke quietly to the assembly, now interrupted by often noisy responses to the slave's cry.

"It is true that many are physically in bondage. Do not fret. It does not impinge on your loyalty to the truth. If you can honestly gain your freedom, do so. If you cannot, then be content with your physical lot. But be free—free in spirit. Christ offers that freedom. If the Son of God makes you free, you will be really free."

After more discussion and more speaking by Paul, the meeting began to break up. Onesimus slipped out of the hall, interested in talking with Epictetus, but anxious lest he be recognized by any of Paul's friends. He had seen Epaphras, Luke, and Timothy. He hoped they had not seen him.

But at the evening meal Paul broached the subject with his friends, leading to a discussion primarily with Epaphras.

"Was that the slave of Archippus at the back of the hall today?"

"I did not see Archippus. I suppose he is busy making the move to Colossae."

Epaphras, lately returned from Colossae, had not had a chance to bring Paul up to date on developments.

"Archippus has completed the move to Colossae, but Onesimus fled from Laodicea. His master set up a search, primarily in Colossae and perhaps in Hierapolis. Surely Onesimus has not come to Ephesus. If so, what is he doing? Where do you suppose he is living? Insofar as I know, he is not a believer. Why would he show his face to those of us who know him to belong to Archippus—to those of us who know and love Archippus?"

"My vision may be dim, but I'm almost certain that Onesimus was in the hall today. We won't say anything to Archippus except to make some inquiry. The young man may need help. He may need some friends. By the way, has Philemon decided to stay in Laodicea and host the church there?"

"Philemon has become a strong leader in the Lycus Valley. His business success has allowed him time to study and to lead others in studying the Scriptures."

8

Timothy set out the next morning on the search for Onesimus. He knew of Paul's eyesight problems, and he wasn't at all sure that the slave had been at the previous afternoon's meeting. Yet, he made some discreet inquiries and learned that two young men were recent arrivals and were living in the back of silversmith shops. He was not so well known in Ephesus as was Paul, so he visited the first shop as a prospective customer—at least, the shopkeeper took him for a customer. While he talked with the smith he caught sight of a young man in the backroom, busily engaged with finishing off a silver image of the temple.

"I see you have an assistant."

"He's an apprentice and is doing quite well. Would you like to see him at work?"

Timothy responded positively as they moved back of the table where the wares were displayed and into the next room.

"Sure I would."

"This is Alexander, a promising young craftsman."

Hearing the courteous introduction, Alexander rose to his feet out of respect for the visitor. So confident was he in his youthfulness that he felt no fear or suspicion.

"You seem to be making great progress and fine images."

Timothy felt a bit uncomfortable in complimenting him for making idols.

"I can see that you are profitably engaged. Do you know of a young man who might be willing to help me with some personal things—cleaning, painting. . .?"

"Yes, I have a friend who might help you. He works for Demetrius in a shop down the street, but he has more free time than I have."

Timothy thanked them both and moved toward the shop where Onesimus worked, managing the place while Demetrius was away. As soon as Timothy walked in he recognized Onesimus, and Onesimus him. They greeted one another warmly, though Onesimus knew that his freedom might be in danger. Yet he remembered Paul's words about freedom of the spirit, so he faced Timothy.

"Paul thought that he saw you at the back of the hall yesterday and was anxious that I see if I could find you. Are you alright? Do you need anything? Do you need a friend—like me?"

"Of course, I need a friend. You know me, and you undoubtedly know what I'm doing in Ephesus. Before you judge me too harshly, though, tell me what you know about Julius and Claudia."

"We'll have to ask Epaphras about that. He has been to Colossae most recently."

"I heard Paul speak again about freedom. He teases me with his ideas and his words. I want freedom, and except for any search on the part of Archippus I have achieved it."

"Let me take you to Paul tonight," Timothy urged.

"To Paul, yes, but not to Archippus. Agreed?" Onesimus bargained.

Meanwhile Demetrius and some of his friends had visited the magistrate with a complaint against Paul.

"This fellow is a Jew, and you know we have accused Jews of robbing temples in Ephesus to support their temple in Jerusalem. This fellow Paul is encouraging non-Jews, native Ephesians, to send gifts to Jerusalem. He says it's for the poor there, but we suspect it's for the temple. We charge him with the crime of temple robbery."

It was a serious charge and one that a civil magistrate, especially in Ephesus where the civil-religious ties were strong, could not take lightly. So, the officials placed Paul under house arrest and prevented him from speaking in the Hall of Tyrannus for several days.

"Temple robber! Me? I would rob the temple alright—of its human slaves and its slavish sex-worshipers. But its funds I would not touch."

Paul fumed at the charge to his companions. As they were eating the evening meal, Timothy came in with Onesimus.

"Onesimus! Son, where have you been? What are you doing here in Ephesus? How did you get here? Does Archippus know where you are?"

Paul's delight in seeing the young man overflowed in a series of questions, the last of which proved somewhat troubling. He allowed Paul's embrace and returned it but felt uncomfortable with these friends of Archippus. To be sure, he had violated the law in running away from Laodicea. But he did not intend to return, and the reference to Archippus set him a-bristling.

"I am a runaway slave. No man has a right to own another. I have heard you say as much, Paul. I have now achieved the freedom you promised me. I do not intend to give it up."

Luke and Epaphras had said nothing but seemed glad to see Onesimus. Paul was put on the spot. He had talked about freedom. Now an escaped slave whose owner he treasured as a friend stood before him. He would be true to the truth he proclaimed.

"No one will force you to return to Archippus. You are welcome to stay here with us. Our quarters are ample, though I am confined to them—thanks to Demetrius, the silversmith."

At the mention of Demetrius, Onesimus was alert.

"Is that the Demetrius whose shop is near the temple?" asked Timothy.

"Yes, he and some of his friends accused me today of robbing the temple. And, you know how serious that charge is in Ephesus."

"That's where I found Onesimus."

"And that's where I have been working and living."

Paul and his friends arranged for Onesimus to move out of Demetrius' shop and in with them. Onesimus gave no real reason to Demetrius for the move; the shopkeeper charged it off to the transience of youthful workers.

Onesimus did not see Alexander for several days, causing Alexander to wonder if his friend's master had found him and taken him back to Colossae. He finally asked Demetrius about Onesimus, and Demetrius told him as much as he knew.

Although Paul hoped to resume his discussions in the Hall of Tyrannus, he was not allowed to leave his dwelling. During the period of his house arrest and with the necessary presence of local peace officers, Paul and his friends felt that Onesimus ought to stay somewhere else.

Paul had met in Corinth several years previously Aquila and Prisca, a tentmaker couple by trade who maintained a shop in Ephesus, so he arranged for Onesimus to stay with them. They were kind, hard-working, and committed Christians. Although he had never worked with the coarse fabric used in making tents, Onesimus learned quickly and proved quite adept.

He learned to use the rough cloth, woven from the plentiful supply of goats' hair, to make tent hangings or to form the outer tent. Paul himself had been trained in the craft and was pleased that Onesimus had responded so readily to it.

"It's time to rest a bit."

Aquila's words were welcome to the young man, weary from the painstaking needlework.

"It's also time for a bite to eat."

This word from Prisca was even more welcome. Fruit and bread made up a hearty snack. The older couple did not know much about Onesimus, having taken him into their home solely on Paul's recommendation.

"Tell me, where is your home, Onesimus?" Aquila asked as they relaxed.

"My home is in Lystra," he quickly replied.

"Then how did you come to Ephesus?" Prisca asked innocently.

Onesimus did some fast thinking.

"I heard Paul preach there, and I was attracted to his gospel."

"But you are not a believer yet, are you?"

"No, perhaps before too long."

The conversation was mercifully shortened by the appearance of a man a few years older than Onesimus but younger than Aquila. Aquila welcomed him and introduced him to Onesimus.

"Rufus is a faithful Christian. Indeed, he could hardly be other than. Tell him, Rufus; tell him about your father."

Rufus had told the story many times.

"My father's name was Simon. We lived on the outskirts of Jerusalem for a short time. Father was a native of Cyrene. He was returning to Jerusalem from a field outside the city one spring day when Roman legionnaires seized him and compelled him to bear a burden. That is not unusual in Jerusalem, but this burden was a cross made of wood. He joined the procession near Jesus, who was being taken to Golgotha to be crucified. And there's the story: My father, Simon, bore Jesus' cross to Golgotha. Not willingly, to be sure, but he sensed Jesus' innocence and godliness. A short time after Jesus' resurrection he joined with the apostles and other friends to await the miracle of Pentecost."

Some of the information was unfamiliar to Onesimus, but he stood in awe of Rufus. He had a direct contact with this Jesus. Onesimus needed to talk with Rufus!

Paul, becoming increasingly restless in his house-prison, had sent Epaphras back to the Lycus Valley to strengthen the believers. He came first to Laodicea, where he found an enthusiastic group of worshipers in the house of Philemon.

Philemon had matured as a believer, having gained access to copies of the Jewish prophetic writings and then studying the materials. He not only provided the meeting place for the church but also served as its leader in study and worship.

"Epaphras, had I known two years ago how fulfilling this fellowship and ministry would be, I would have pursued Paul to Ephesus and brought him here. We want him to come and teach us and visit with us."

The visitor from Ephesus smiled wryly but then shared Paul's situation with his host.

"I'm sure nothing would please him more, but he's under house arrest for temple robbery. Can you imagine? Paul wouldn't be caught dead in the temple of Artemis—though with his reputation in Ephesus, if he were caught there, he might as well be dead."

"Is he in any immediate danger? Ephesus is a hot-headed, hot-tempered city. The tide of bigotry might well turn on him and the other believers—perhaps turn from the Jews to Paul and his followers."

"He does not appear to be in any immediate danger. He's only inconvenienced, but that's danger insofar as Paul is concerned. Perhaps he will be free to visit Laodicea and Colossae and Hierapolis before too long. Tell me about the group in Colossae."

Philemon hesitated for a moment. Apphia, his wife, brought in tea and cakes. Epaphras stood when she entered the room, and the two exchanged greetings.

"The work in Colossae is making progress, but Colossae is such a strange town. Most of the folks are religious, but not particular. Any god or goddess, any law or laws will do, just so long as they pretend to be religious. They prefer legalism to freedom. They prefer to work their way to their gods rather than accepting the work of grace from God. And this is true with some of our group too. I have tried to keep close watch over the church there. It's meeting in the house of Archippus. Archippus is a good man, but he's so involved in business affairs that he has little time for the church."

At this point Epaphras interrupted Philemon.

"Already the hour is late. Perhaps I ought to make my way to Colossae."

"Stay here for the night. Get a fresh start in the morning."

And so Epaphras and Philemon dined together and talked together until well into the night—Paul and his ministry, the faith at Laodicea, the church in Colossae, Archippus and his household. Interestingly, they said nothing about Onesimus. It was as if he did not exist. Of course, he had not identified with the group of believers, and Philemon did not know him well.

Early the next morning Epaphras set out for Colossae. He promised to return if possible, through Laodicea. Philemon wanted to know his reaction to the situation in Colossae and to Archippus.

On arriving in Colossae, Epaphras asked directions to the house of the wool merchant Archippus. He soon found the house. Archippus had sent Julius to the door, as the servants were busy inside and outside. Julius was elated to see the visitor.

"Welcome to our home. We had heard that you might come. Father will be so glad to see you. Tell me about Timothy and Dr. Luke and Paul. We now have a church meeting in our house, though we do not have a regular teacher."

Epaphras, struggling to get a word in edge-wise, enjoyed the chatter from the 13-year-old but signaled for a brief interruption.

"How is your father? How are you?"

"We are fine, but it's not the same without Onesimus. I still don't have a tutor, and I miss my friend. Have you seen him or heard anything about him?"

The subject of Onesimus was a no-no. Epaphras had been pledged to secrecy, so he simply ignored the question by Julius.

"Please call your father."

Julius was quick to do just that. Archippus came from his private quarters and warmly greeted Epaphras with an embrace.

"Good friend, it has been some months since we saw you. You bring us news of the gospel's spread, I trust. Here we are reaching out to much of the city. Not all of them understand the meaning of God's grace, but we are working on it."

"Ah, not all of us understand the meaning of God's grace, but we are living in it. Tell me, are you free to talk, or should I come back at another time?"

Epaphras did not feel so comfortable with Archippus as he had with Philemon. Was it because of something that Philemon had said about the faith in Colossae? Or was it because Archippus owned Onesimus and Epaphras knew where he was?

"Why don't I call Julius and ask him to entertain you for an hour or so. I have some business commitments I need to discharge, but then I'll have the rest of the day with you. We'll meet for lunch, but it's time now for you and Julius to enjoy a mid-morning snack. There's so much we need to talk about. We need your help. I need your help. We need a spiritual leader such as Philemon here. I already depend on him a great deal."

Having said this, Archippus summoned Julius and went back to his business.

Julius led Epaphras immediately to the kitchen and snack area. Julius' appetite had never been satisfied, and he took this need seriously. Claudia and Poppae were both happy to see the visitor and arranged some goodies for him and Julius. Julius was still a household favorite. Claudia had news.

"You remember that the master gave me my freedom. He has been most helpful in finding me a job outside the household, although he has assured me that I'm welcome to stay on here. A friend of Paul in Philippi has a purple-dyeing business. She is a native of Thyatira, and she and Archippus have had some business relationships. She wants to open a branch of the operation here, and the master has recommended that I help in its beginning. I'll have to learn a great deal, but he has promised to guide me. We open up in about a month."

Epaphras had never heard such a long speech from Claudia, and she had probably never made such a long one. He was pleased.

"Are you enjoying the study and worship here in the house?" he asked.

She assured him that she died. By this time Poppae had rejoined the conversation. Her kitchen duties had taken her attention for a few moments.

"Frankly, we both miss Onesimus."

Julius affirmed Poppae's feelings.

"We all miss Onesimus. It's almost as if the household, so lately moved from Laodicea, has lost its heart and enthusiasm. I haven't been in a scrape or even merited Father's rebuke for months. Claudia, you and I need to go fishing or climb a mountain or rob a fruit stall or something."

"I'm all for it. Now that I am free, you and I could liven up Colossae the way you and Onesimus livened up Laodicea. But he had such original ideas for getting into mischief. I do miss him. Where do you suppose he is? Is he in trouble? Is he in good health? I think Archippus misses him too!"

Epaphras simply listened, wanting to reassure them, yet not daring to share information on the runaway slave. Fortunately, they knew nothing of his being with Paul in Ephesus. Perhaps there would come a time when Epaphras could tell them.

Lunchtime came and Archippus joined them in the dining room. Poppae stayed with her duties in the kitchen while Claudia served the meal and then, daughter-like, sat at the table with them. By this time several others had come in—members of the somewhat disorganized group of believers. Epaphras had met some of them. One weird-looking man came in. Epaphras thought he might be an astrologer, but why would he share in a Christian meal and meeting? He introduced himself as Astrallus.

Astrallus had developed a superstition about astrology. He respected the stars and their movements. He supposed there might be powers in the air that controlled or at least affected human behavior. To him, God—or a god—was all powerful, but he wasn't absolutely sure as to the place of God's son in the order of things. This, Epaphras learned in an initial conversation.

Being careful not to stir up controversy in the group, Epaphras spoke positively about the deity of Christ and the complete sovereignty of God. Archippus agreed but seemed unwilling to make an issue of it with Astrallus. Epaphras wondered cynically if there was a business connection.

It was clear in the discussion Epaphras led that the group lacked a closely-knit agreement on important issues. Another person came to the meeting, also somewhat of an outsider. He had been strongly influenced by the Jewish faith. Epaphras knew there were many Jews in the valley, and he knew something of the hostility toward them. He was surprised, however, to hear the newcomer speak.

"We ought to plan a new moon celebration. God's people have long worshiped him in the new moon. I am shocked that people who call themselves

God's people do not carefully observe the practices that history exemplifies. And another thing: it seems to many of us that we should be meeting on Sabbath eve instead of the first day of the week. Remember that God gave the command to Moses, 'Remember the Sabbath day to keep it holy.' We are not going to reach out to Colossae unless we are faithful to God's law."

When Ezra—his preferred Jewish name—had finished speaking, Epaphras concluded that Colossae was indeed a variegated city and the church appeared to be equally so. He also agreed that the nature of the worship and study experience was clearly informal. Indeed, it lacked leadership. Archippus was not the right person for this leadership. While Epaphras was musing on these matters, a younger man stood to his feet.

"Epaphras has taught us well. We serve the God who made heaven and earth—and who yet controls them. He has called us to identify with his son and with his church. By God's grace and not by the old law . . . by God's majestic power and not by the powers of the air . . . we are saved and sustained. As our Lord was raised from the dead, so let us enjoy new life in him, believing and behaving as his people."

"Who is that young man?" Epaphras asked Archippus.

"Oh, he's something of an idealist. His name is Tychicus."

Epaphras thought he sounded rather realistic and resolved to talk with him. The discussion continued until almost everyone had had his say. Archippus attempted to make a closing statement, but it lacked something of clarity and courage. Epaphras returned with Archippus to his home, and there they sat, eating and talking about the church in Colossae and its needs.

Epaphras spoke first.

"The positions supported by Astrallus and Ezra are not Christian. God in Christ has overcome the powers of darkness. God in Christ has fulfilled the law. Now by grace we live and in love we serve."

"I know that, and I have tried to lead the church in truth. But the move from Laodicea, which I made for the sake of the church, taxed my business. I sacrificed my home in Laodicea and have opened my doors to the meeting of the church. What have I got for it? A missing slave! Onesimus wasn't the hardest working person in the household, but he was good for Julius and I paid a good price for him. If I get my hands on that boy. . ."

It was just as well that Julius came into the dining area at that time. Archippus would not alienate his son by bad-mouthing his slave. Julius wanted help with a problem in composition. His teacher had made the assignment, and Julius had learned to turn to his father for help since Onesimus had fled. Epaphras marveled that the boy was so quiet and respectful—a promising lad!

Then he noted an opportunity of ministry that the young churches should enjoy.

"You know that Paul is continuing to receive an offering for the poor in Jerusalem. And you know that's the reason he's under house arrest. I'm not sure whether Colossae has considered this matter. Philemon assured me that Laodicea is storing up some funds for this purpose. You can depend on Philemon for spiritual leadership. He and Apphia love the Lord, and their home is a good witness."

Archippus responded apologetically.

"I sense that our group of believers is not maturing. We lack leadership. I have neither the time nor the ability. If there were someone here who could assume that role, it would be great."

Epaphras was impressed with the forthright statement in the group.

"How about someone like this young man Tychicus? I'm not sure he's old enough—mature enough—but he is a clean-cut young fellow."

"Age has little to do with it. No one despises another for being either too young or too old."

Epaphras pressed his point further.

"I'd like to talk with him—perhaps tomorrow."

It was growing late, so both Epaphras and Archippus were ready to conclude the conversation. Tomorrow would be another day.

The next day Archippus sent for Tychicus, and the three men talked about the Good News and the church. Epaphras and Tychicus were both committed to the sort of leadership the church needed. Tychicus promised to take a more active role in insuring the progress of the church.

Epaphras planned to return by way of Laodicea. He visited with Philemon for a few hours. They talked frankly about Archippus and the variety of beliefs in the church at Colossae and about Tychicus, whose discovery Epaphras considered the high point of his visit.

9

An unexpected turn of events was afoot for Paul and the spread of the Good News. Junius Silanus, proconsul of the province of Asia, had befriended Paul shortly after Paul arrived in Ephesus and had attended several of the meetings in the Hall of Tyrannus. Although a man of sluggish nature, Junius was the great-great-grandson of Emperor Augustus. He also was the cousin of Nero and thus in constant danger even before Nero became emperor. Because Asia was a senatorial province, he represented the senate.

When Junius heard that Paul had been charged with the crime of temple robbery he called for an inquiry. Realizing that Paul was innocent of the charge, he engineered the lifting of house arrest and visited Paul to tell him he was now free to continue his teaching.

Onesimus was with Paul when the proconsul came. He was introduced simply as a member of the household. The guards were dismissed, but not without a word of appreciation from the prisoner for their considerate treatment. He spoke lightheartedly in his new state of freedom while also challenging Junius.

"I tried to make believers out of them, Junius, but they were afraid you would dismiss them as being soft touches if they became Christians."

"I would treasure their new moral standards if they became a part of your group."

"Then why don't you become a sharer of the Good News?"

Onesimus was more caught up by the challenge than was Junius. Why not? He had experienced the friendship of Paul, Timothy, Luke, and Epaphras—even beyond the loving care of those in Laodicea, now in Colossae. After Junius and his officers left, Onesimus talked with Paul about the faith.

"You are almost ready, Onesimus."

"Almost? What's to keep me from joining with you?"

"You are not your own. You must relate properly with Archippus."

At that clear reference to his slavery and Archippus, Onesimus flushed and slipped out of the house. He made his way to the house of Aquila and Prisca, who knew nothing of his slave status. Perhaps he could lose himself in making tents. He felt rejected by Paul.

Epaphras returned to Ephesus, high in the praises of Philemon and Tychicus but entertaining some question about the stability of Archippus and Colossae. Onesimus managed to corner him and ask about his friends Julius, Claudia, and Poppae, for whom he was deeply concerned.

"Are they happy in Colossae?"

"They are settling down. Julius misses you especially. Your friendship was most helpful to him. He's growing up into young manhood."

"How about Claudia? Has she made any plans for her newly gained freedom?"

Epaphras noted a different tone in his voice and suspected that more than mere friendship was involved.

"She plans to enter the business of purple-dyeing in which Lydia of Thyatira and Philippi has been so successful. Archippus is interested as a wool merchant. Some of the white wool of his sheep will lend itself beautifully to the dyes."

"Will she remain in Colossae?"

"Yes, she plans to remain in the house of Archippus though her business will be semi-independent of his affairs."

"And Poppae, how is her health?"

"She appears to be strong. There is no better cook. Even with my family in the area, I am drawn to the kitchen of Archippus."

Suddenly shouts outside the hall attracted their attention. Always there was noise in the streets, but this was different. It was as if a mob, newly formed, might be swarming down the way. The crowd was only gathering at the hall and Paul had not yet appeared. Epaphras recognized the signs: young men running together, officers of the law pursuing them, older men—shopkeepers, craftsmen—following. In the open area outside the hall the young men, upwards of a hundred, turned to face their pursuers.

"We're going to be free."

"No man can own another."

"You've no right to our service."

"We'll die for our freedom."

Soon the chant became deafening.

"Freedom, freedom, freedom."

The few officers and other pursuers could only stand accusingly, awaiting further help.

About this time Paul approached the hall from another direction. Sensing the danger in the confrontation, he called for quiet and was able to defuse the explosion—much to the dismay of the officers and the owners, who fired back at him.

"Of course, you are called to freedom."

"What do you mean, troublemaker?"

"All men and women are free in Christ Jesus. Respect one another. Honor your freedom."

"They aren't free. They're slaves. They're our property. I paid hard cash for three of them."

Onesimus was standing clear, unwilling to identify himself as a slave but conscious of the crisis. He recognized Alexander, whom he had not seen in some weeks, among the hangers-on—neither with the slaves nor with their pursuers. Onesimus wondered why the slaves did not continue their flight. An open fight appeared probable.

Some of the officers unsheathed their weapons and were advancing on the slaves. A thrust of a blade drew blood, and the riot took on new life. The offending officer was immediately taken by the slaves and thrown to the ground. He was about to be crushed when the sound of approaching horses signaled the end of the trouble. Well-armed troops moved in, producing a great deal of head-knocking and more bloodshed. The large number of slaves were huddled together and then marched off to face the authorities and to be restored to their masters. Why had they not continued their flight?

Onesimus learned that the slaves had come to the Hall of Tyrannus seeking help from Paul, but he had been unable to aid them. Paul was one to talk about freedom, but hardly a realist. He talked and did nothing. Onesimus was yet resenting Paul's reference to his own slavery and his responsibility to Archippus.

Alexander spotted Onesimus, and the two of them watched sadly as the soldiers herded the slaves away from the hall.

"Onesimus! I thought your master might have reclaimed you. Where have you been hiding?"

"I haven't been hiding. I've been helping Paul and his friends."

"Oh yes, I've heard about him. My master, not my slave-master mind you, blames Paul for a drop-off in business. He seems to be discouraging the purchase of offerings for the temple. Tell me about him."

Onesimus didn't care about discussing Paul.

"Tell me about yourself. Are you almost ready to go into business on your own? Have you developed your skills? Any news from Colossae? My former master has now moved to Colossae."

"No news from Colossae. I don't want to hear anything from that situation. I am living free—that's for me."

They spoke in muted tones as they continued talking about their masters in Colossae. As Paul began to speak, Onesimus invited Alexander to join him in his usual back seat of the hall. For a short time the two sat together and listened. Then Alexander made some excuse about having to report to the shop and left Onesimus alone in the crowd. Still, it was great to have seen Alexander again. He was his first friend in Ephesus.

As Paul spoke again about Christian freedom, Onesimus shuddered at the status of the slaves who had so recently gathered nearby.

Did he have no more security than they? Should he have joined the riot? Was he a coward to hang back? Why could he not be as courageous as Paul, twice imprisoned already in Ephesus, or Timothy or Luke or Epaphras?

Onesimus suffered the comparison as he remembered that he too had a master. While he mused over the situation a young man approached and sat down nearby. There was a lull in Paul's teaching and movement in the gathering. The two young men stepped out on the street together, and Onesimus spoke in a friendly fashion.

"My name's Onesimus."

"My name's John Mark."

"Have you heard Paul speak before?"

"Oh yes, I was with him several years ago when he first left Antioch in Syria with Barnabas."

"Why, that's when I first heard about him—when he came to Lystra. Were you with him in Lystra? Isn't it beautiful?"

Onesimus began to wax eloquent about his home.

"No, I left Barnabas and Paul and returned to Jerusalem," Mark, a bit apologetically, replied.

"Oh then, you missed Lystra. Why did you go back to Jerusalem?"

"I'm not sure. Perhaps I was homesick. Perhaps I was disillusioned about my part in the mission. Perhaps I resented Paul taking the leadership away from Barnabas. But I know that Paul did not understand. He and Barnabas split up over my departure. Paul thought I was a quitter. And I suppose I was in a sense. Anyhow, I'm planning to talk with him."

Onesimus saw a bit of himself and his own cowardice in Mark. He recognized that Mark was committed to the cause and had turned back. At least he himself was not committed to the cause—or Paul.

Timothy caught sight of Mark and approached. When he learned who he was, he realized that he had taken Mark's place on the first mission. Now the three men were conscious of the ties that entangled them. Paul saw the trio and rejoiced to see John Mark.

"Mark, my son, how are you? Welcome to Ephesus. Will you be here for awhile? Come to my house. We need to talk. Onesimus, you and Timothy bring him after this next session."

Paul returned to his place at the front of the hall. Onesimus and Mark returned to their place at the rear of the hall.

"If God so loved us, we ought also to love one another."

Paul had now directed his teaching to ethical issues.

"Those who are believers in Judea are in great need. Many times their non-believing countrymen discriminate against them. The weekly dole is withheld from the believers. Business relations have been interrupted. As they shared with us their spiritual blessings, let us share with them our material blessings."

This plea sounded logical to Onesimus and Mark; they understood his point of reference. Jesus had lived and died in Judea and Galilee. The first group of believers gathered in Jerusalem. They had spread the Good News to surrounding territory, and the church at Antioch in Syria had actually sent Paul and Barnabas out as its spokesmen.

Onesimus and Mark were a bit surprised, however, when Paul summoned them to stand at the door with baskets to receive an offering for the saints.

"Young men, you who sit at the rear near the door, will you stand there and hold a basket apiece so that these friends may share their gifts with the suffering saints in Jerusalem? Then in time we will appoint some representatives to take the gifts to Jerusalem."

Onesimus and John Mark immediately complied with the request, and the crowd began to leave the hall. There were two older men present who did not appear to fit in with the others and who departed rather abruptly. Onesimus and the others did not notice them, but the two men quickly made their way to another meeting already in progress.

Demetrius appeared to be in charge and was speaking, followed by others in the group.

"We've got to do something. My sales were off by half last month, and I blame Paul for my loss."

"My shop in Laodicea has almost no business, and I understand Colossae is also feeling the pinch."

"But Paul has not been to those places, has he?"

"No, but his influence is felt throughout Asia. This is the chief city of the province, and we are guardians of the temple."

With difficulty Demetrius regained control.

"If we do not do something immediately, our business will be ruined and, more importantly, the worship of the great goddess Artemis will be sorely affected. All the world worships Artemis. Are we to allow a little Jewish rabble-rouser to destroy her?"

"But what can we do? Paul has broken no law. We tried before to move against him, but he suffered no penalty worse than house arrest."

"And the proconsul lifted that after a few days."

"We have just come from the Hall of Tyrannus where we heard Paul ask his crowd to give gifts for Jerusalem. He dares take gifts from Ephesians who treasure Artemis. He dares suggest that these gifts be sent to another temple—in Jerusalem."

The two men had finally had their say.

The men were joining in the discussion so despairingly that Demetrius summoned them to silence.

"Let's plan a huge assembly in the theater tomorrow. We'll take Paul and his friends before the Artemis-worshippers themselves. The mob will deal with them."

With that concrete suggestion he dismissed the artisans, firm in the belief that they could work up a crowd on the next day.

10

So it happened that the artisans began to gather with the worshipers around the Temple of Artemis. Some, remaining in their shops, spoke with their customers.

"You know that the worship of Artemis is being threatened? Yes, that's right—as much as Artemis means to Ephesus."

"These Jews, not natives of Ephesus, always criticize us for our worship. We believe Artemis came down from heaven, a gift from Jupiter himself. They defy us by saying they worship not idols made by hands. In addition, that troublemaker Paul is their chief spokesman."

Soon there gathered little groups near the temple, a magnificent structure—one of the wonders of the world with its Doric columns, finely etched stones, and bejeweled mortar. From the groups intent on conversation three words stood out: Artemis, Jews, Paul. Some of the priests came out to join the groups . . . How had they found out about Demetrius' plans? Eunuchs all! The priestesses/prostitutes—always a welcome addition to conversational groups—also joined them.

Artemis was threatened! This maiden-huntress deity represented the chase to be sure, but more importantly represented reproductive power for both human and animal life. Her working power was recognized all over Asia in all life—plant and animal—making her worship by prostitution logical. Some considered her the mother of life; the guardian of young people; the goddess of childbirth, war, the sea, and the moon.

Her Roman name was Diana—that is, the Romans included a Diana in their pantheon who resembled Artemis. Artemis was threatened—and her worship—and her worshipers.

Soon the little groups gathered together and the street was filled. Now Demetrius took charge of his craftsman cronies, explaining in a voice loud enough for others to hear.

"Men, you know that great Artemis is worshiped all over the province of Asia and elsewhere. What you may not know is that a little Jew named Paul has discouraged many worshipers. Why, he describes great Artemis as an idol made with hands. Certainly our trade is in jeopardy, but more importantly, the sanctity of our goddess is in danger."

Onesimus and two of Paul's companions, Aristarchus of Thessalonica and Gaius of Derbe, were on their way to the Hall of Tyrannus when they heard the disturbance. They drew near the crowd to hear in more detail. Demetrius, who had not seen Onesimus, spoke accusingly.

"Artemis may be dethroned from her position of protectress of all Asia."

When the crowd heard this threat to their beloved goddess, they began to cry out.

"These Jews, not natives of Ephesus, always criticize us for our worship. We believe Artemis came down from heaven, a gift from Jupiter himself. They defy us by saying they worship not idols made by hands. In addition, that troublemaker Paul is their chief spokesman."

Others took up the cry until Onesimus and his friends realized a riot threatened. Before they could do anything about it, however, they felt themselves being prodded along by a thousand bodies in the direction of the huge theater. And all the time the crowd sang, chanted, and shouted, "Great is Artemis of the Ephesians."

The enthusiasm was seasonal. Each year, as a part of activities to honor Artemisia, the temple and civic authorities sponsored games. But now something special was happening, and the crowds sensed it. The closer they came to the theater, the louder the cries became. The crowd increased in size and intensity. Gaius, Aristarchus, and Onesimus had not yet been recognized by those near them and simply flowed with the traffic. They could do nothing else.

Meanwhile Paul had reached the Hall of Tyrannus and heard the din of voices. He inquired as to its source. When told that a riot was in the making, he sensed that his teaching time would be interrupted. With several of his regulars he began to follow the noise. Soon he was able to make out the cry, "Great is Artemis of the Ephesians."

Paul first supposed the cry referred to the celebration of the annual feast. While he and his companions walked toward the crowd, two friends—both of them asiarchs—met them.

"Paul, you must not go to the theater. The city is in an uproar. Some of them are screaming for your blood."

"All I have heard is the name Artemis. I'm sure I have nothing to do with the idol and the temple."

Paul was a Roman citizen and valued the respect that such worship involved. He did not consider the emperor divine, but he knew that the myth was a valuable tool of peaceful administration. He and the asiarchs were on friendly terms, and they considered him an ally for good government. They were not so sure about the unethical standards of the leaders in the cult of Artemis, however.

By this time Paul and his group were following the crowd more closely and saw that they were entering the theater. His friends pleaded with him not to enter, then physically restrained him and removed him from the scene.

"This is no time for a brave pronouncement. This crowd is after blood—anyone's blood. Let it not be yours."

Inside the theater Demetrius and his artisan allies, instigators of the riot, had dragged Gaius, Aristarchus, and Onesimus to the stage. When the crowd saw them, although they did not know them, they shouted all the louder, "Great is Artemis of the Ephesians." Yet some shouted obscenities and threats against those who dared to challenge the greatness of their goddess.

"Jews, Jews, Jews," some of the crowd cried.

The Jews had been so insistent in their monotheistic teaching that many of the Ephesians could not separate them from any others—philosophers who denied the existence of all gods. The Ephesians had heard that Paul was a Jew and now that Paul's companions were on display on the stage, they supposed that all the Jews of the city were involved. The fact that neither Gaius, Aristarchus, nor Onesimus was a Jew did not occur to them.

But there were Jews present in the assembly, many of them herded along as were Onesimus and his friends. They feared for their freedom, their business interests, and their lives. They pushed a certain one of them, Alexander—not the young man who was a friend of Onesimus—to the stage. He stood there with the others and then moved to the center as he attempted to quiet the crowd, gesturing with his hands. Demetrius spoke as he pointed to him.

"Jew, Jew!"

At this point the crowd went completely out of control. Some raised their fists, some surged toward the stage, some jumped up and down in their frenzy, but all cried aloud, "Great is Artemis of the Ephesians."

The search for Paul that some had initiated was forgotten in this new fanaticism. All of the hostility toward the Jews—their high moral standards, their insistence on the worship of one god, their faithfulness to their own religious institutions—all of this opposition came to full vocal expression. Strangely, no one was physically injured. Apparently, Demetrius and his friends had sought to avoid any act that would make them liable to punishment.

But Onesimus did not know that. He knew only that he was suffering as a friend of Paul's and that he had been mistaken for a believer, for a member of the church in Ephesus.

What honor was there in suffering for a right that was wrong—or at least that was wrongly understood? Where was Paul? He was glad enough that his friend was nowhere to be seen. This was no place for Paul!

For two hours in the theater the crowds shouted, "Great is Artemis of the Ephesians! Great is Artemis of the Ephesians!"

Onesimus, on the stage all of this time, grew increasingly uncomfortable.

Finally, another man made his way through the crowd and up on the stage. He too signaled for silence. Only with great difficulty did he quiet the crowd. Demetrius and his friends backed away from him as he took center stage. They knew him to be the town clerk. Demetrius had seized an opportunity for a noisy minority of Ephesian citizens to take control. Now his scheme was about to be defeated as the town official spoke.

"Men of Ephesus, everyone knows that Artemis is great. Everyone knows that Ephesus is the center of her worship and the keeper of her temple. Everyone knows, all over Asia, that her image in the temple is the gift of Jupiter himself. Now since these things are true, why don't you stop yelling? Be quiet, and do not do anything rash. Why don't you shut up?"

The crowd listened to this affirmation of their faith.

"You have dragged these men up here who are not temple-robbers. Nor have they blasphemed our goddess. You have verbally attacked a respectable Jewish citizen, Alexander. These three men are not Jews."

Demetrius and his friends were making for the steps that descended from the stage when the town clerk turned toward them.

"If then Demetrius and his fellow craftsmen have anything against any man, there is a proper procedure for making charges. The courts are open, and there is a proconsul. Let this matter be considered legally. And if any of the rest of you have a complaint or a problem, let it be settled in the regular assembly. We have meetings of the assembly three times each month. I'm in charge and you come before me."

Even then the assembly was slow to break up, with feelings yet running high. Onesimus, Gaius, and Aristarchus, though freed by the outcome, were reluctant to leave the stage and mingle with the crowd. Demetrius and his friends were nowhere to be seen after the town clerk's rebuke.

Onesimus didn't sound too brave at this point.

"I was scared. There must have been 25,000 people here—this place was filled. You couldn't see any of the white in those marble seats. And the stage was filled too."

"That crowd had murder in their eyes—and I was looking through their eyes at a few frightened members of the church," Gaius added.

Aristarchus joined in the conversation.

"Well, I'm not officially a member of the church, but I intend to talk with Paul tonight. Anyone who has 25,000 enemies out to get his blood can't be all wrong."

His logic was a bit shaky by some standards, but the quality of the hostility was as convincing as the quantity.

"Did you see how they railed against Alexander?"

"Yeah, I felt sorry for him and for all the Jews. It's not their fault."

"If anyone's to blame, it's Paul and the rest of us who work with him. I'm glad to know that Artemis and her religio-economic combination are hurting."

"That's quite a word, 'religio-economic.' I've heard of the religio-politic combination in Philippi. I suppose this is the same general outfit."

The three young men were responding with some degree of nervousness, and it was difficult to sort out the speakers. Now that the press of the crowd was less intense they made their way to the town clerk who had been talking with some of the crowd on the stage. Gaius addressed him with appreciation in his voice.

"Sir, thank you for rescuing us. We didn't know what might happen with that crowd."

"They came to an orderly position rather quickly. That's usually true when their leadership backs off. No damage done? Good. I'm glad that Paul was not present."

Where was Paul? Prevented from joining the others in the theater, he had been encouraged to return to his lodging place. There he awaited a report on the assembly. Late in the afternoon news began to drift in: The riot was over—just a noisy disturbance—and none of his friends was mistreated. Then the asiarchs and the town clerk came to the house where he was staying.

"Paul, we are placing you under house arrest for your own protection. If you had been in the theater today, they would have pulled you in two."

"Wait a minute. I have my work to do. I need to be at the Hall of Tyrannus every day. My mission depends on my daily teaching."

The town clerk responded to Paul's protest.

"Your mission depends on your staying alive. There were 25,000 persons gathered in that theater today and they aren't happy over the outcome. Don't you see, Paul, that this house arrest is for your own good?"

"No, I don't. Not at all! I'm a Roman citizen, and you are unduly and unjustly limiting my freedom. I object."

"Because you are a Roman citizen, we have an obligation to protect you. It is our opinion that we can best do that by confining you to this house.

Your friends can visit with you. If anyone wants information about your mission, that person can come here to ask you."

So the Ephesian authorities decided that Paul would once again be confined to his house. He calmed down a bit when Onesimus, Gaius, and Aristarchus brought him a firsthand report. Timothy and Erasmus had been sent to Thessalonica and Philippi a few days before the riot. That meant the three young men were the primary objects of the mob when they identified them with Paul. He listened as they recounted the day's events. Later, tired out from the excitement, Gaius and Aristarchus went to their quarters. Although Onesimus had been staying with Aquila and Prisca, he lingered to talk with Paul.

"Paul, you know that I have been interested in becoming a disciple. You have sensed that I was on the verge of commitment. After being forced to stand up for the church today, I am now ready to be identified with it."

Paul was overjoyed, but he remembered their previous conversation.

"That's fine, Onesimus. You have been profitable to me since coming to Ephesus. I remind you, however, that you are not your own. You belong to Archippus."

Onesimus had already considered that relationship.

"I know that I belong to Archippus. I am ready to return to my master and endure slavery for the Lord's sake."

"My son—for you have become my son in these months—I will write Archippus a letter explaining the situation and asking him to be considerate. You are going back willingly, and you have matured considerably. Surely he will be merciful."

"Whether he is merciful or not, I know that I must return."

Paul confirmed his plan regarding the letter. His limited activity provided him with time to write carefully, so he chose his strategy with Onesimus in mind. He would write to Archippus at Colossae but send the letter along with Onesimus and Tychicus, a faithful Christian, to Philemon at Laodicea. Philemon could then be counted on to recommend consideration of Onesimus, as Archippus looked to Philemon for spiritual leadership. At the same time Paul would send a letter to the church at Colossae, a church that desperately needed a word of wisdom and encouragement. The one would be a personal letter and the other a church letter.

11

The church in Colossae had critical needs. Without a strong spiritual leader, the believing group had not had the advantage of a consistent teaching ministry. As a result, both their Christology and their commitment were at fault. A bit of secular philosophy had been welcome, as was always the danger in a predominantly Gentile church. All of this led to questionable ethical standards.

Carefully, Paul wrote to the needs of the church. Tychicus and perhaps Onesimus were closely enough related to Paul that they could clarify any matters the letter might stir up.

Beyond individual behavior there was a need for societal standards to be elevated: Relations between husbands and wives were to be redeemed from the male tyranny that so often characterized them. Wives were to be "in subjection" to their husbands, but husbands were to "love their wives." Children were to be obedient, but their fathers were not to abuse them. Slaves were to "obey" their masters, but masters were to be "just and equal" toward their slaves.

At this point Paul had in mind the plight of Onesimus and the right of Archippus.

In the last paragraph of the letter to Colossae Paul mentioned Onesimus.

"I am sending Tychicus, beloved brother and faithful minister and fellow servant in the Lord . . . together with Onesimus, the faithful and beloved brother, who is one of you."

At this point in the writing Onesimus became a bit shaky.

"Paul, should you refer to me in so similar a vein as to Tychicus? No one will accept me as a brother—least of all in Colossae."

"Of course they will. Colossae, Laodicea, and Hierapolis are closely related —and a resident of one is a resident of the entire Lycus River Valley."

"I know you aren't a name-dropper, but could you sorta mention a few of our friends? They are my friends too."

"That sounds like a good idea. How about bringing in Aristarchus and Mark and Justus? Then I'll mention Epaphras—he's one of your friends.

Luke you know well. I'll mention Demas too. There is a group meeting in the house of Nympha. I'll mention that group."

"But, Onesimus, I want you to read this last suggestion. See how this sounds to you."

Onesimus read with great excitement.

"And say to Archippus, 'Take heed to the ministry that you have received in the Lord, that you fulfill it'."

"That's straightforward from my standpoint. Do you suppose my old master will take offense at it? Will he get the point of 'the ministry that you have received in the Lord'?"

"Oh, I don't doubt he will recognize my frame of reference, especially in light of the letter I intend to write to him personally in care of Philemon. He'll understand what 'ministry' I mean—the acceptance of you as a brother."

Paul closed the letter with only a brief reference to his imprisonment.

"Remember my bonds."

In one sense it was easier to write the longer letter to the church than the one addressed to Philemon and Archippus. "Paul, a prisoner of Jesus Christ"—that was important to Archippus, who knew how much Paul cherished his freedom. Little wonder that Paul himself did not visit Colossae! "And Timothy, our brother"—everyone at Colossae thought highly of Timothy. Tychicus was a brother, Onesimus was a brother, and Timothy was a brother. Onesimus wondered at the address, "to Philemon, our beloved and fellow worker, and to Apphia our sister."

"Paul, how is this going to make Archippus feel? Will he take offense at Philemon and his wife receiving the letter before he does?"

"Son, you have to do this sort of business right. I am appealing to Philemon for help. I am appealing to Archippus in the name of the fellowship. I am not violating a confidence."

It did seem strange, addressing the principal person in the dramatic confrontation third in order, "to Archippus our fellow soldier."

"I hope this doesn't ruffle his feathers. He's a powerful businessman."

Paul replied, "He is also a powerful Christian, and I'm reminding him of those ties in this other address, 'and to the church in your house'."

"Then it's another church letter."

"No, it's a personal letter. I'm just reminding him of our gratitude for his deep involvement in the mission and reminding him of the 'ministry' I mentioned in the church letter. The usual greeting will suffice: 'Grace to you and peace from God our Father and the Lord Jesus Christ'."

"I've never been the subject of such an appeal before. I suppose I'm embarrassed at your going to such trouble in my behalf."

"Onesimus, Onesimus—profitable you have been to me personally. I want to secure your freedom, but I want Archippus to free you willingly."

The initial prayer of thanksgiving and the brief play on mutual relations demonstrated good epistolary style, and Paul was a past master at writing letters:

> *I thank my God always, making mention of you in my prayers, hearing of your love, and of the faith that you have in the Lord Jesus, and toward all the saints; that the fellowship of your faith may become effectual, in the knowledge of every good thing that is in you, unto Christ. For I had much joy and comfort in your love because the hearts of the saints have been refreshed through you, brother.*

Even so, Onesimus marveled at Paul's eloquence—writing of love and faith and fellowship. If Archippus could only be encouraged to live up to his past record . . . yet it's easier to talk of love and faith and fellowship than it is to talk of giving a runaway slave his freedom. How was Paul to broach the subject? So far, he had skated around the edge of the inevitable request.

"Look here, Onesimus. I'm not going to mince any words. I'm going to remind Archippus that it is right for me to request him to free you, but I'm not going to demand that right. It's an appeal based on love—his love for me, our love for Christ."

"Paul, wouldn't it be easier on all concerned if I just stayed here in Ephesus or went to Philippi or Corinth rather than for you to put so much pressure on Archippus? You are really sticking your neck out."

"Read this: 'Wherefore, though I have all boldness in Christ to demand that you do what is right, yet for love's sake I rather ask, being such a one as Paul, the old man, and now a prisoner of Christ Jesus . . .'"

"I can't believe it. You are laying it on the line. If Archippus doesn't respond to what is right, on the basis of love, to a request from an old friend, an old man, and a prisoner—then he rejects completely your friendship."

"That's about it. I'm making the appeal as strong as possible. I want Archippus to set you free."

"You have been like a father to me, Paul. You have put up with my growing pains and my irresponsible flightiness. I am grateful for what you are doing. I'm just not worth it. Onesimus may be my name, but I've been unprofitable to everyone I've known for the past months."

Paul continued writing for a moment and then handed the pen to Onesimus,

"Here, you write this request: 'I beg you for my child, whom I have begotten in my bonds, Onesimus, who once was unprofitable to you but now is profitable to you and to me, whom I have sent back to you, Onesimus, that is, my very heart'."

"I'm grateful that you consider me your son in the faith. I'm grateful for your friendship."

Onesimus was overcome and fought back the tears. Yet he wasn't ashamed of those tears with Paul. But how could he face Archippus—even with this letter?

Paul continued to dictate.

"I would like to have kept him with me so that in your behalf he might minister to me while I'm a prisoner for the gospel. But without your knowledge I would not do anything, so that your goodness should not be of necessity but of free will."

Onesimus understood that he was to be the testing device for Archippus' Christian commitment. Did he resent it? Did he feel a bit apologetic or even sympathetic for Archippus? After all, he had been a kind master and Onesimus had acted irresponsibly—even before his flight. Now he found himself stricken by Paul's kindness, conscience-stricken by his own flight.

He sought to remember the attitude of Epictetus toward freedom and his own logical defense of human freedom. And how could he write, even at Paul's dictation, of a goodness of free will rather than of necessity? He had little goodness of either variety!

There was no let-up in Paul's free word flow.

"For perchance on this account he was separated for an hour that you might have him back forever, no longer as a slave but more than a slave, a beloved brother, especially to me, but how much more to you both in the flesh and in the Lord."

Paul had called Onesimus "brother" in the letter to the church. Now he asked Archippus to accept him willingly as a brother. He could not be slave and brother at the same time. And all of this interpreted as Paul's understanding of Providence. It was beyond the reach of Onesimus. If the faith could work this transformation in master-slave relationships, it could transform all human relationships . . . a "brother" both "in the flesh and in the Lord."

"If then you hold me as partner, receive him as myself. And if he wronged you or owed you, charge this to my account."

Onesimus was writing carefully. He had not stolen anything from Archippus when he fled. Well, there was a bit of food from the kitchen, but certainly he wouldn't begrudge him that pittance. And there was the horse, but Onesimus planned to reimburse Archippus for the animal. Of course, Hector and Justus might have plotted against him and blamed him for some theft they had engineered. He wasn't looking forward to seeing them again. What if Archippus assigned him to the stables?

Then he remembered: He belonged to Archippus by right of purchase and had removed himself. Could that be theft by taking? Was that the point of Paul's reference?

While he was musing on these matters Paul spoke. At first Onesimus thought he was dictating, but then realized he was being addressed.

"Give me back that pen and paper, Onesimus. I need to write this in my own hand. This is a business transaction."

Onesimus remembered the use of one business term. "Perchance on this account he was separated for an hour that you might have him back forever" . . . That verb "have him back" was used in receipts: "receive him in full."

Paul took the pen and began to write.

"I Paul write in my own hand. I will repay it."

It was a promissory note. Paul assumed the debt—any debt—that Onesimus owed to Archippus. He continued to write.

"Though I might say to you that you also owe me your own self."

As Paul read it aloud, Onesimus questioned him again.

"How was that? Archippus owes you some money?"

"I did not say anything about money. I wrote that he owed me himself. I shared the Good News with him. I have encouraged him in the faith. I think he owes me something."

Onesimus had not considered that possibility, but he did remember how glad his master had been to see Paul and how he rejoiced in his decision to become a believer. Many people had played on the meaning of his name, Onesimus. Some had considered him profitable, others unprofitable. Now it seemed Paul played on it in his next remark.

"Yes, brother, let me have profit from you in the Lord. Refresh my heart in Christ."

It was almost as if Paul had made an investment in Archippus and wanted to collect his interest. Onesimus acknowledged the investment Paul had made in his own life and was more than willing to pay the interest, but Archippus? He wasn't sure his master understood his relationship with Paul in terms of money.

Paul continued writing, and Onesimus felt more comfortable. He spoke aloud before he wrote, apparently being quite conscious of any possible misunderstanding that might develop.

"Having confidence in your obedience, I write to you knowing that you will do even more than I say."

Onesimus shuddered at the word "obedience." He had never thought of his master's obeying anyone—and now Paul was confident. It was true that Paul had not actually requested Archippus to free Onesimus, but this left no room for doubt: that's what Paul meant—I know that you will free Onesimus. A tingle of hope swept over his person. . . If Paul is confident, I dare hope.

Paul was so caught up now in writing that he seemed to ignore the younger man's presence. Yet he mouthed the words as he wrote.

"At the same time prepare for me a lodging, for I hope that through your prayers I shall be granted to you."

Had it been anyone else, Onesimus would have been amazed at the gall of the man. It was as if Paul were saying, "You'd better do what I ask. I'm coming to check up on you soon. Make ready a room. I'll stay at your house—with the church that will certainly know all about this business. And all of this in answer to your prayers."

Onesimus wondered how Paul knew the object of his master's prayer. Under similar circumstances, the young man thought, Paul would be the last person he would want to see—especially if he had not granted his request. Again, there was that tingle of hope. Paul just might pull it off.

The closing salutation was the normal one—except that by now Onesimus was reading between the lines. He didn't suspect Paul of skullduggery: Onesimus had come to recognize Paul's persistence and his determination to accomplish his purpose.

"Epaphras, my fellow captive in Christ Jesus, greets you . . . Mark, Aristarchus, Demas, Luke . . . my fellow workers."

What a powerful list that was. From Epaphras, who had first brought the good news to the Lycus Valley, to Luke, the beloved physician who had brought Julius back to life: these two with three others sending their greeting. It was as if all of the influence of these friends piled up to accomplish Paul's purpose. Could it be that they all knew of Paul's intention? Had Paul talked of his hopes with all of his friends? And how about this threefold reference to Paul's imprisonment? Was that fair?

"Remember, I'm a prisoner for the Lord."

Certainly not even Onesimus viewed with suspicion the benediction, "The grace of the Lord Jesus Christ be with your spirit."

What a letter! It was brief but to the point. Indeed, Onesimus questioned whether such a powerful appeal could be expressed in so few words.

But the letters were only the beginning of the problem for Onesimus. He was now under obligation to face Archippus—and Julius and Claudia and Poppae, friends whom he had deserted when he escaped. What would they think? Could he rekindle the flames of friendship?

12

While Tychicus and Onesimus were preparing to go to Laodicea and Colossae, Paul was released from house arrest. The asiarchs and town clerk felt that the danger to his person had lessened. Before the riot in Ephesus, Paul had planned to return to Macedonia and Achaia and later to visit Jerusalem and then Rome. His plans had now changed. From Macedonia and Achaia he would go to Laodicea and Colossae as he had indicated in his letter to Archippus. He was busy preparing for the offering he hoped to take to the poor in Jerusalem.

The time came quickly for Tychicus and Onesimus to set out for Laodicea and Colossae. In addition to the friends of Paul in Ephesus, Onesimus wanted to say goodbye to one other person: his first friend in the city, Alexander—a runaway slave like himself. The two young men became close friends during the early days before Onesimus had moved from the shop of Demetrius to the lodging of Paul. They had talked occasionally after that but moved in different circles.

Onesimus walked to the shop where Alexander worked. He had made good progress in his apprenticeship. Onesimus admired his work, though viewing its model distastefully. Alexander greeted him warmly.

"Onesimus! It has been a while. Tell me about yourself."

"I've made a big decision, and I want to share it. But what about you? Are you enjoying your smithing?"

"Yes, but not as much as I anticipated. There isn't much variety to challenge me, and the customers are for the most part older folks. I miss you and don't have many friends. What's this big decision you've made?"

"Alexander, I'm returning to Colossae and my old master, Archippus."

"You're a fool, man! Has he caught up with you? Did he send a search party? I'm sorry."

"You don't understand. I'm going back willingly. I've become a believer and he's a believer, and this is right for me."

"He'll beat you and starve you and torment you. The law sets no limits on his treatment of a runaway slave. You're a fool!"

"Whatever he does to me he will be doing to his own property. I belong to him and I intend to pay that debt."

"Well, I don't suppose I'll see you again because I'm certainly not going back to Colossae to visit my former master. It's goodbye then. Take care of yourself."

The two embraced and Onesimus was gone. Alexander sat down on his workman's bench and shook his head.

So Tychicus and Onesimus set out on the road to Colossae.

"Tychicus, am I a fool to return to slavery?"

"It is unusual, Onesimus, but I wouldn't call you a fool. You apparently agree with Paul that it's the right thing to do. You do the right thing and no one calls you a fool."

"But someone did, and I have doubts about my own good sense. What if Archippus does not respond to Paul's letter in a kind way?"

"I have read the letter addressed to Philemon first and then to Archippus—and I have read the letter addressed to the church in Colossae with its closing appeal to Archippus. I cannot imagine his denying Paul's request."

All the way from Ephesus to Laodicea Onesimus was anxious. He had so enjoyed his freedom. He could hardly think in terms of slavery again. The several-day journey was uneventful, and they drew near to Laodicea. It was growing late, and neither Tychicus nor Onesimus felt comfortable about barging in on Philemon and Apphia in Laodicea. About 15 miles out from the town limits they came up on an inn and decided to spend the night. When they pulled up to the courtyard a handyman met them and helped them dismount from their horses.

The travelers found welcome in warm food and a room with two cots. Early in the evening their weariness became sleepiness. Tychicus fell asleep immediately, but Onesimus tossed about a bit.

What if Archippus deals with me as I deserve?

Onesimus knew the penalty levied on runaway slaves—and he was a runaway slave. He thought about the demonstration in Ephesus and the Roman troops that moved in with their clubs, beating the slaves unmercifully. He had heard about imprisonment and cruel torture. Slavery as an institution was legal, protected by the legionnaires.

A noise outside caused Onesimus to jump up from the cot and open the curtain a fraction. Had they traced his progress and come to seize him? Nothing appeared in the courtyard, so he lay down again and tried not to disturb his roommate. He dozed off and began to dream—of Hector and the stables. Hector held a huge whip menacingly and began to threaten Onesimus. Behind him, smiling, or rather leering, his approval was Archippus.

"So, you thought to escape. Boy, you are in trouble."

Other slaves moved in and bound him, leading him off toward prison. As the prison doors opened, he awoke with a start and cried out.

"Help me. Oh, help me."

Tychicus stirred in his sleep but did not awaken.

Throughout the night, every time Onesimus closed his eyes he imagined danger.

What if the letter and Tychicus together do no good? What if Julius has turned against me—I couldn't blame him? What if Claudia reported my advances to her and the entire household is against me? What if soldiers have been posted to seize me even in Laodicea?

When daylight began to break, Onesimus wearily turned toward Tychicus. Then shortly after dawn Tychicus awoke and called cheerily to him.

"We are almost there, Onesimus. You will soon see your friends. And we hope you will soon have your freedom."

"I wish I were as hopeful as you seem to be. I have been awake most of the night worrying."

"Worrying? What have you been working yourself up about? Don't you know the authority with which Paul has written—veiled, to be sure, but real?"

"I've been thinking about slavery and what owners can do to runaways, and Tychicus, that's what I am—a runaway!"

Tychicus reassured him.

"You are more: You are a child of God. You are a valuable person. You are a friend of Paul."

"I know that, but does Archippus know? Will he accept me or punish me? What does my future hold?"

"Let's take one thing at a time. We'll stop by Laodicea and talk with Philemon. With him on our side, we'll be in a good position to approach Colossae and Archippus and Julius."

Tychicus did not know of the dreams Onesimus had of Claudia.

The two men left the inn after enjoying a light meal, guiding their mounts toward Laodicea. As they came in view of the Lycus River Valley, Onesimus thought increasingly of his months in the area. And, his thoughts turned to Claudia and to Julius.

He had made a fool out of himself in his advances to Claudia. What must she think of him—or did she even think of him at all? He sensed a yearning for her that might be love. But she was free and he was returning to slavery.

He thought of Julius, the young lad who had become such a good friend. He supposed that he had led him astray or at least had not sought to stem his disobedience. He knew Julius had grown. How old would he be? About 13? Onesimus was 19. He had grown too in the months at Ephesus—and had matured in other than physical ways.

The travelers made their way to the house where Philemon and Apphia lived. A servant met them at the door and led them into the front parlor. Soon Apphia arrived, welcoming them and promising that Philemon would soon be home; he had gone to visit a member of the church in Laodicea who was ill. Shortly he entered the room and was both surprised and glad to see Onesimus and Tychicus. After exchanging greetings he immediately asked Tychicus about Paul.

"I heard that he was under house arrest again. Is he well? Is he free yet? Is he yet in Ephesus?"

"He was under house arrest following a noisy demonstration in the theater, but now he is free. He was leaving Ephesus for Macedonia and Achaia when we left a few days ago."

"Tell me about yourself, Onesimus. You fled from the household of Archippus many months ago—about the time he moved to Colossae. Has he freed you? If not, you are in grave danger. I know that he sent out searchers. In any event, I am glad to see you. I have heard that you are now one of us—and I welcome you to the church. But we must address the slavery issue."

Tychicus sought to interrupt this speech several times, and finally spoke.

"I have a letter addressed to Archippus in care of you and Apphia. Paul hoped that you would read it and pass it along to Archippus with your recommendation. I have another letter directed to the church in Colossae that refers to it, urging Archippus to do the right thing."

"Let me see the letter addressed to Archippus."

Philemon took the letter from the hand of Tychicus and began to read,

"Paul a prisoner of Christ Jesus, and Timothy our brother, to Philemon our beloved and fellow worker, and to Apphia our sister . . ."

Both Tychicus and Onesimus waited anxiously as he read. When it became apparent that Paul was requesting freedom for Onesimus, Philemon reread a few sentences. When he finished he looked into the eyes of Onesimus.

"You will never have a better friend than Paul."

"I know that, and I am grateful."

Tychicus wasted no time in his purpose.

"Now, Philemon, do you agree with the rightness of Paul's request? Are you willing to make a note on the letter indicating that you urge Archippus to free Onesimus? Or, will you write a third letter?"

"It is clear that Paul is asking Archippus to set Onesimus free. I wonder if I ought to interfere. To put it bluntly, Paul has gone to Macedonia and Achaia and left this responsibility for me to assume. I have to live near and work with Archippus. He may very well resent this letter from Paul."

Apphia now spoke for the first time.

"It is true that relations between owners and slaves are better among believers. Philemon, this will be an opportunity for an owner to be both gracious and good. The example may be far-reaching. No one of us feels comfortable owning slaves. Surely we could free them and pay a living wage for service rendered."

"Apphia, you are letting your tender heart get ahead of your tough brain. Too much of our economy is based on slavery. Yet, you are right and Paul is right. Onesimus must be set free. At the same time, it must be the willing decision of Archippus. Yes, I will write a note to Archippus."

Philemon to my friend and brother, Archippus:

Your slave, Onesimus, is returning willingly to you. Paul has written a letter asking you to receive him as a brother. He has meant a great deal to Paul, and he can mean a great deal to us. I urge you to take advantage of this opportunity to be both generous and good.

Greetings from your friends in Laodicea

With that letter in his possession to bolster the chances that Onesimus would be freed, Tychicus bade farewell to Philemon and he and Onesimus set out for Colossae. They reached the outskirts of the neighboring city when their fortunes turned, however. Onesimus saw them first: several of Archippus' herdsmen and their overseer Hector. Immediately Hector and two of the herdsmen converged on Tychicus and Onesimus.

"So, boy wonder, you thought you could get by with escaping. We figured you were somewhere close by. Our master will be pleased to see you. There's no telling what he has planned for you. Come with us. We'll take you to Archippus."

Despite protests from Tychicus, Onesimus was rudely taken and the four men moved off toward the house of Archippus. Tychicus followed closely, hoping that Onesimus would not be mistreated. The long search for the runaway slave was at an end. Onesimus had been recaptured.

While Onesimus was taken to the stable area of the compound, Tychicus approached the entrance. There he sought admittance and was greeted by a household slave. When he identified himself, he was ushered into the large room at the front of the house. There, after a longer time than usual, Archippus met him. He was apologetic about the delay.

"Tychicus, I'm so glad to see you. I would have come more quickly, but I just got word that a runaway slave has been apprehended. He actually ran away from my house in Laodicea, and we have sought unsuccessfully to find him. Now the slaves will take care of him. Strange how they resent a fellow slave who has managed to escape. Ah, but tell me what brings you here. And how is Paul? And the others—Timothy, Epaphras, and Luke?"

Finally, Tychicus was able to reply.

"Archippus, Onesimus returned with me. He has been in Ephesus with Paul and agreed willingly to accompany me and return to you, his master. He has become a believer and has been a real help to us in Ephesus."

Archippus was shocked.

"Do you mean that my slave has run away to Ephesus, met some of my close friends and fellow Christians, and no one of you told me about it? What sort of friendship or fellowship in the faith is that? He is my property, and you have used him without my permission or even my knowledge."

Tychicus was surprised at the anger of Archippus and decided this was a good time to give him Paul's letter.

"A part of the explanation you will find in this letter that Paul has addressed to you in care of Philemon. And Philemon has written a brief note as preface to it. I also bring a letter from Paul to the church here at Colossae that I believe meets in your house."

Archippus resented his friends taking advantage of him. He was a hard-nosed businessman and had been generous with Paul and his work and with the local church.

"A letter from Paul, eh?"

He took the letter with the note from Philemon and began to read. The words from Philemon did not set well with him. His dealing with Onesimus himself had been interrupted by the announcement of the visit by Tychicus, and he had not even seen the slave. He began to read the short letter from Paul. It affected him strangely.

Tychicus observed Archippus closely—"fellow soldier," Paul the prisoner for Jesus Christ called him. His countenance was a mystery. Surprise, resentment, remembrance, puzzlement, thoughtfulness: all of these registered in an occasional smile and a frequent frown.

"What does Paul expect me to do: free Onesimus without any punishment?"

Tychicus was silent for a moment.

"Onesimus is now a brother, Archippus. He has ministered to Paul and his friends in your behalf. He returned willingly. I trust that you will be merciful in your handling of this situation."

"Mercy or justice? You realize that I have other slaves."

"Yes, and some of them you have freed. You are to be congratulated on their emancipation."

"But Onesimus fled my household just when I was about to realize through selling him my original investment in his purchase."

"Father, I think I saw Onesimus out in the yard. Hector and a couple of others appeared to be roughing him up. Surely you won't let them mistreat him. He's my friend, regardless of the fact that he ran away."

Julius rushed into the room, speaking loud and fast. He paused when he noticed that his father had a visitor. He apologized to Tychicus and to his father but continued.

"I have missed him and I for one am glad for his return, but please don't let Hector and the others hurt him in any way."

"Julius, go out to the yard and tell Hector that I said he is to release Onesimus. Then, you bring him to me."

Julius was gone in a flash of adolescent haste, and Archippus returned to his conversation with Tychicus.

"You see something of my quandary: I am angry while my spiritual father and my physical son both plead for a runaway slave."

With a wry grin on his face, Archippus took the hand of Tychicus—who immediately foresaw the outcome. While there in the house of Archippus, in the room where the church met for worship, Tychicus handed him the other letter, the one Paul had addressed to the church at Colossae. He began to read it as Julius led Onesimus into his owner's presence. Tychicus and Julius faded into the background as Archippus accosted Onesimus.

The slave had been buffeted about a bit by Hector and the others but, except for the disarray of hair and clothes, appeared none the worse for wear. He bowed to Archippus and then fell on his knees as the drama of the moment hit him. Archippus reached out and pulled him to his feet.

"Onesimus, once you were profitable to me. Then you became unprofitable. Now I accept you as a brother or a son. You are free to go or to stay. Julius joins me in the hope that you will stay and be profitable to both of us and to the church that meets here in the house."

Onesimus was overwhelmed. His wildest dream for months had been fulfilled. He thanked Archippus profusely. The two embraced warmly, and then Julius began to whoop it up! He grabbed Onesimus in a typical young teenager's burst of enthusiasm, oblivious to the presence of the other two men.

"Now you can really be my brother. We'll have a great time together. We are both older, Father, and we will behave more maturely. You'll see."

With that ill-considered promise, Julius and Onesimus headed for the kitchen.

"Archippus, you really did it. You honored Paul's not-too-subtle request, and you fulfilled your son's dream. I am certain that Onesimus will prove profitable once more. This is Friday. Will the church meet here day after tomorrow?"

Archippus, himself a bit shaken by his decision, holding the letter to the church in his hand, answered in the affirmative.

"Yes, and I will read Paul's letter to the church gathered here—that is, unless you want to read it. I'll keep his letter to me personally. Perhaps someday Onesimus would like to claim it as his own."

Tychicus felt a genuine affection on the part of Archippus for Onesimus, and he felt as if his mission had been accomplished.

Julius led Onesimus straight to Poppae who, dropping the pot of gravy in her hand, hugged him lovingly. She surveyed the gravy, the floor, and the pot—in that order—before speaking.

"It's worth more than a pot of gravy to have you at home."

Julius blurted out the news.

"Poppae, he's free. Father freed him, and he's going to stay with us. Aren't you, Onesimus?"

"Yes, if you and your father want me to stay, I would be happy to do so."

"Do you have some of those little cakes Onesimus likes, Poppae?"

"Of course. I have some that I have just baked—but, as I remember, you like them as much as Onesimus."

"Well, yes, but Onesimus is our guest and I will defer to him."

In mock solemnity he bowed and pointed out the cakes to Onesimus. The all-too-recently-freed slave missed a presence in the kitchen but decided to say nothing about Claudia. He was with friends, and for a few moments the months in Ephesus receded as if he had never left. How good God was!

13

Saturday dawned clear and warm. Onesimus and Julius had stayed up quite late on Friday night. Indeed, it is questionable whether either had slept. Conversation extended through questions and answers, reports on friendships, lifestyles, and life philosophies. Julius was filled with questions, and Onesimus had many answers.

"Tell me about Ephesus. Did you go to the Temple of Artemis? We had a great time together there. What sort of job did you find?"

"Now that's two questions. Yes, I went to the temple with a new friend. We did not dare go in. The crowd outside was large and rude—not worshipful, I'd say. But then I'm sure they were not there to worship the way we do. I found a friend on my way into town, Alexander. He was my age and also a runaway slave—from Colossae."

"Has he returned to his master?"

"No, and I don't think he will. He's an apprentice to a leading silversmith, and he enjoys both Ephesus and his work."

"What did you do? How did Paul find you, or how did you find Paul?"

"I worked in a shop for a few weeks. It wasn't difficult to find Paul. Wherever there was trouble, there was Paul. The Jews didn't like him. The business interests didn't like him. The temple crowd didn't like him. So, he was always stirring up trouble—or so it seemed."

"Julius, tell me about yourself. You must have grown a foot. How are your lessons? And have you gone on any more hiking trips—or have you found anyone foolish enough to go with you?"

"You can certainly tell that I have matured into a serious and dignified young man. And you must know that since you left I have mastered the science of studying. I haven't had a rebuke from my tutor in months. Nor have I disobeyed my father in any detail since you have been gone. Indeed, I might almost say that your departure was the best thing that could have happened to my academic and family life."

Onesimus playfully slapped him on the shoulder.

". . . And the worst thing that could have happened to your personal enjoyment! Well, I've missed you too. I wanted to write a note, but I knew that would be a dead giveaway to your father. Fortunately, Epaphras visited Colossae and brought me news."

"To answer your question about my visits to the mountains and the river, I must confess that I've stuck pretty close to home since we moved to Colossae. I've made a few friends, but I haven't had anyone to encourage my mischief or to cooperate therein."

So it went through the night, two young friends renewing their friendship after many months apart. The morning meal was always an event at the table set by Poppae. Julius and Onesimus were early participants, arriving at about the time the early slaves were leaving. Archippus came in before they finished their meal and seemed happy to see the two together again. Then he spoke to the older lad in a serious but relaxed tone.

"Onesimus, I'd like to talk with you this morning. No hurry, but could we get together about mid-morning?"

"Certainly. I'll meet you. I look forward to catching up on the news."

Relations were not so tense as when the one was master and the other slave.

Onesimus met with Archippus. The situation appeared to be relaxed. One problem loomed for the younger man, however. How was he to address his former owner? "Sir" would be a start.

"What's your opinion of Julius? Has he made any progress? Does he appear to be interested in his studies? I had trouble with him after you left. It was a terrific adjustment—losing his best friend and moving to Colossae within a short span of time."

"Sir, I am impressed at his self-confidence and his ability to communicate. Of course, the two of us never had any trouble communicating. At the same time as I have matured, Julius also has matured."

"I hope you will help him as you have done in the past. I love him dearly and want him to grow up into clean and capable manhood. He has drawn near to the church since it has been meeting in our house, but he has not committed himself to membership. I'm sure your example will be a powerful one."

"I hope to take my place in the church here. Paul and our other friends came to mean a great deal to me, and I enjoyed the group of believers."

"We meet tomorrow, as you know. I want to have Tychicus read Paul's letter to the church, though I think I will not read my letter from Paul aloud."

Onesimus remembered his first response to that letter and was glad Archippus would not read it.

"Would you like to add a word about your relationship with Paul—and your relationship with the church in Ephesus?"

"Yes, I would like that opportunity for a brief statement. These friends may not know me—certainly they do not know the new me. I have something I want to say."

"I have been troubled about the church. Philemon has encouraged us, but I haven't had time to do much. I hope you will become an active witness in Colossae."

"I can't preach or teach like Paul, but I'm a part of it, and I'll talk about it wherever I go."

"From Paul's letter to me by way of Philemon, I think he plans to come by for a visit. I sensed a bit of pressure on me to free you and then for him to come and check up on me. That's Paul for you. He certainly doesn't mince words."

"He left Ephesus on a brief tour of Macedonia and Achaia. The church at Philippi was so generous with its gifts that he wanted to visit it. Thessalonica and Berea were clamoring for a visit too. There has been a fair amount of misunderstanding with the church at Corinth. I don't know what has got into them. But Paul has promised a visit whether they are glad to see him or not."

"How long do you suppose that will take? When can we expect him?"

"Oh, I'd say it will be several months—perhaps a year. He had indicated that he might like to visit Illyricum, and that may extend the time."

"Oh yes, you will be interested to know that your friend Claudia is an independent businesswoman. We couldn't offer her much more than a servant's role here. I had some connections with Thyatira and learned of Lydia, a merchant of purple dyes and of purple-dyed stuff. Then I learned that she was a friend of Paul at Philippi and a faithful Christian. Lydia is an independent businesswoman, and when I broached the subject to Claudia she jumped at the opportunity. With my help and encouragement, she has opened a shop here in Colossae and business is quite good."

"I remember Claudia well. I hope she has forgiven my impetuous actions in the dining area before I left."

"I'm sure Claudia bears no grudges. She is a lovely and mature young woman."

"In any event I hope she will be at our meeting tomorrow."

"I think you can count on that. She's another Lydia where the church is concerned—strong leadership material."

The conversation closed on the same note of relaxed friendliness with which it began. The miracle of transformation had been accomplished: master and slave had become brothers.

Although Jews set aside Friday night and Saturday for their worship, the church regularly met on the first day of the week. For the most part these meetings were arranged for the evening, as most worshipers worked during the daytime hours. The service on the first day of the week celebrated the event of the Resurrection—also occurring on the first day of the week.

The worshipers began to gather at dusk. Many of the women brought dishes of food. Onesimus looked forward to the tasty morsels prepared by the ladies of Colossae. He knew that Poppae was also preparing for the love feast that would follow the meeting, the teaching and preaching.

When about 25 people had gathered and begun to make themselves comfortable on the cushions scattered over the floor, Onesimus became aware of the hum of low conversations. He had stood at the door with Archippus and Tychicus, welcoming those who came. He knew some of them, but not so many as if he had been in Laodicea. Claudia had not come when he and Tychicus left Archippus at the entrance and found themselves a cushion apiece.

The hum of conversation seemed to be changing and then, almost imperceptibly, became the hum of a tune. Soon the words were recognizable:

> *How amiable are thy dwelling places, O Lord of hosts!*
> *My soul longeth, yea, even fainteth for the courts of the Lord.*
> *Yea, the sparrow hath found her a house, and the swallow a nest*
> *For herself, where she may lay her young,*
> *Even thine altars, Oh Lord of hosts, My King, and my God.*

It was a hymn Onesimus had enjoyed in Ephesus. The Jewish Psaltery was a ready source for devotional reading and for singing. Fortunately, since Onesimus could not read Hebrew, it had been translated into beautiful Greek many years previously. Other psalms and spiritual songs followed. He could not tell who was leading them—perhaps the singing was spontaneous. Much of the worship at Ephesus had been free and relaxed. Paul's teaching lent order to the service.

Then came a period of praise and prayer. Again, he could not determine the leader. There were objects of prayer mentioned and then someone would begin the petition, "Oh, Lord, our Lord, how excellent is thy name in all the earth."

As others entered the room, out of the corner of his eye Onesimus saw a vision of loveliness walk quietly into the group of worshipers. My, how Claudia had matured. No longer was she the serving girl in the dining area at Laodicea. She was a beautiful, gracious young woman.

Archippus began to speak after the murmur of praying voices had subsided. He introduced Tychicus as the bearer of good news from Paul. Tychicus began to read the letter.

"Paul, apostle of Christ Jesus through the will of God, and Timothy our brother, to the saints and faithful brethren in Christ at Colossae. Grace to you and peace from God our Father."

Immediately the attention of the worshipers turned to Tychicus. Most of them had not met Paul, but they knew of his work. Timothy they had met along with Luke and Epaphras. Paul had addressed a letter to Colossae! The believers listened to the reading without interruption, down to the last sentences.

"And when this letter has been read among you, cause that it be read also in the church of the Laodiceans; and that you also read the letter out of Laodicea. And say to Archippus, 'Take heed to the ministry that you have received in the Lord, that you fulfill it'."

Here questions began—almost before the final "grace be with you." What about the letter out of Laodicea? Who has it? And the "ministry" that Archippus received—what was Paul writing? Yet the hum of puzzled voices was subdued. Tychicus deferred to Archippus, who in some embarrassment sent Julius to his desk for the letter. Julius returned to hear his father speaking.

"Brothers and sisters, I had forgotten about the personal reference in this letter to a personal letter I also received from Paul. Let me explain. Before we moved from Laodicea to Colossae I had owned a slave, Onesimus."

Onesimus began to feel ill at ease when he sensed what Archippus must say.

"That young man ran away before we moved, and we could not find him. To make a long story short, he fled to Ephesus and there found or was found by Paul. He became a believer and helped Paul and the church there. I knew nothing about his whereabouts for two years. Then, day before yesterday Tychicus came bearing the letter to you and another letter to me—both from Paul. Accompanying him was my long-lost slave."

"My first impression was anger and resentment. I felt that Paul had mistreated me at the least and defrauded me at the most. Then I read the letter he sent to me. Here, allow me to read it."

"'Paul, prisoner of Christ Jesus, and Timothy our brother . . . This letter was sent first to our friends, Philemon and Apphia, at Laodicea. Then, with their approval, it was brought to me. This then is the letter out of Laodicea. You recognize the strong appeal to me to set Onesimus free. Paul not only shared his plea with Philemon but also mentioned it in this letter to you, the church: 'Say to Archippus, Take heed to the ministry that you have received in the Lord, that you fulfill it'."

"I have as of two days ago set the slave Onesimus free. I have fulfilled the ministry opportunity I received. Onesimus is here with us, a free man in Christ Jesus, and a freed man from slavery. Paul asked that I receive him as a brother beloved. Instead I have received him as a son beloved, both by me and my son Julius."

Onesimus arose to speak.

"I am grateful to God and to you for this gathering. I am also grateful to my master/father/friend Archippus. He has been gracious and forgiving. He has indeed given me my freedom. I want to become a useful and profitable member of his household. I want to become an active participant in the work of sharing the Good News. I have much to learn, and you will be my teachers."

Others shared in welcoming Onesimus. But an older member of the group, Leonidus, raised a flag of caution.

"I understand the willingness of Archippus to give his slave liberty, but I call your attention to the fact that many of us hold slaves we will not release. There seems to be nothing in Paul's writing critical of slavery. Indeed, Archippus owns others. Let us be careful not to upset the cart of society and our economic interests."

Archippus responded in a fair but personal way.

"Each of us has the authority and the freedom to release one or all of our slaves. I have released others and look forward to the time when I can release them all."

Then a stern young man spoke up.

"To speak of slaves and freedom is all well and good, but we have talked previously of other more important matters. Why do we not meet on the Sabbath day? Does not the Law prescribe a special day for us to observe? We are violating the Law by continuing to work on the Sabbath—and there are feast days we ought to set aside for exercises of our faith."

Onesimus could hardly restrain himself, but he waited silently as Archippus responded.

"You know that we are not subject to the requirements of the Law. You know that we are free from the Law—as surely as Onesimus is free from me. We observe the first day of the week in celebration of our Lord's resurrection."

The stern young man, who for some reason seemed familiar to Onesimus, spoke again.

"God's law is yet to be obeyed. Some of you are not careful what you eat. Just because a cut of meat is cheap you purchase it—not asking whether it has been offered to idols. And we have almost completely forsaken angels in our worship."

The young man continued in the rut of legalism, a rut Onesimus thought had been filled in Paul's interpretation of the Law. What sort of believers were these in Colossae? He understood now why Paul had written as he had. The church in Colossae had some legalistic elements. Again, however, he did not address the issue.

Others were speaking about the gracious purpose of the Lord, so Onesimus sensed that the legalists were in the minority. He knew, however, how noisy a minority might become.

Archippus began reading the passage of Scripture chosen for study from the prophecy of Isaiah.

"Behold, my servant, whom I uphold; my chosen, in whom my soul delights: I have put my Spirit upon him; he will bring forth justice to the Gentiles. This prophecy was fulfilled in the ministry of our Lord."

Archippus spoke of gentleness, justice, truth, and of courage—all of them gifts from God and available to the believers gathered in his house that day.

Onesimus noted that Archippus did not speak so long as Paul—nor, to be sure, so eloquently. Still he appreciated his emphasis and his interpretation. The time for the close of the service was drawing near. As was their custom, Onesimus learned later, they sang softly the benediction from the Scriptures:

> *The Lord bless you and keep you*
> *The Lord make his face to shine upon you*
> *And be gracious unto you*
> *The Lord lift up his countenance upon you*
> *And give you peace. Amen.*

The softly repeated "Amens" appeared to dismiss the worshipers as they moved from their places toward the dining area. In this movement Onesimus confronted Claudia. She was pleasant and seemed genuinely glad to see him.

"I'm happy that Archippus has freed you. My freedom has been a source of great joy. He has been most generous in establishing my business. We have remained close friends. I yet feel as if I'm a part of the household. Julius is my brother too!"

Onesimus had never seen her so lovely nor heard her speak so graciously.

"May we eat together?" he asked.

"I'd like that," she replied.

They talked as much as they ate. All the worshipers gathered for this agape love feast. It brought the fellowship close together. Onesimus noted that both

Leonidus and the young man were a part. Perhaps there was yet hope for peace on the issues introduced. He asked Claudia who the young man was.

"That's Simon. He came here from Ephesus a few months ago. We had thought he would share the spirit of Paul with us, but surely Paul is not a legalist."

Onesimus remembered when Simon had sought to introduce the same ideas in the Hall of Tyrannus. Paul had disagreed sharply, and shortly thereafter Simon no longer attended the meetings. So he had come to Colosse with his heresy? And there appeared to be no one in Colossae who would openly disagree. Onesimus wondered if he dared confront him on these basic issues.

The crowd began to break up. Claudia said her goodbye and invited Onesimus to visit her business, which he indicated he would like to do. For two years he had not seen her. Now he realized, two years older, that he loved her more than ever. One of the objectives in his new freedom was to win Claudia's love.

14

Onesimus and Claudia did not immediately resume their courtship. Both were busy—Claudia in developing business interests and skills and Onesimus in relationships.

Despite the letter addressed by Paul to Archippus and despite the compliance of Archippus in freeing Onesimus, relationships between the two were often strained. Some tension existed. Although there were no intentional recriminations, Archippus could hardly help remembering. Even the dispatch with which he handled the slave-free issues did not represent a complete solution to the changed relationship. It might have been easier if Onesimus had been freed in Ephesus.

Other slaves in the household did not understand. Perhaps the way to freedom was to be found in running away. Had not Onesimus been forgiven and allowed to go unpunished? Relationships with the slaves who worked outside had never been close. Now Onesimus busied himself with inside activities.

Perhaps no one was happier to see Onesimus "at home" than Julius. Soon Onesimus was helping him with his lessons—not as a slave, but as an older brother. Sometimes he accompanied Julius to class, but most often he merely helped to solve some problem or clarified some explanation. Onesimus was sharpening innate skills in teaching. Both young men took the tutor and his teaching more seriously than before.

Julius frequently suggested that the two of them go fishing, or one of them would occasionally propose hiking up the mountain. Now they approached both from a different angle, and the distance to the mountain at least was greater. Poppae was always ready to furnish a picnic lunch if they chose an adventure.

Sometimes Claudia came to visit Poppae, and when Onesimus would learn of her presence he managed to be there at the same time. It was here that young Julius showed his affection for Onesimus and also his mischief.

Rarely had a little brother been such a nuisance. When Onesimus learned that Claudia was in the dining area visiting with Poppae, Julius also learned of it. He would pop into their conversation, and with mock solemnity remark on the beauty of the day or the latest development in local gossip. Indeed, it was difficult for Onesimus and Claudia to be alone together. Poppae noticed their problem and enjoyed their discomfort, perhaps encouraging Julius in his meddlesomeness. Despite the younger boys pestering, Onesimus and Claudia were developing a beautiful friendship.

Julius was a serious-minded 13-year-old. He had attended meetings where Epaphras spoke and had admired Timothy and Dr. Luke. Now he never missed a meeting of the church in his own house. It seemed to Onesimus that his adopted younger brother was becoming restless during the study and worship sessions. In big brotherly fashion he brought up the subject.

"Julius, you have never made a Christian commitment, have you?"

"No."

The subject might have been dropped there, but Onesimus persisted.

"You have met with believers for several years now, and you are certainly advanced in your knowledge of the church and its beliefs. Aren't you ready to be identified with it?"

"It's true that I have attended worship regularly—my father has seen to that—but you are really the only friend I have in the group. There aren't any boys my age—or girls either for that matter. I would simply be joining a group of adults."

Onesimus picked up on that.

"It's true: there aren't many in our age group. But we are good friends, and I would like nothing better than for you to be clearly on God's side, a member of his church."

He decided this was strong enough an appeal to a younger brother. Julius, caught up in the context of commitment, reached out to take the hand of Onesimus.

"I'll do it—and we'll be the church of tomorrow."

Julius talked with his father, and Archippus talked with him. Satisfied that the young man knew what he was doing, he agreed to present him to the group of believers on the next Sunday.

That day came, and with it a new feeling for Julius—anxious, to be sure, but committed to Christ and his church. The group rejoiced at his decision and took him to themselves—much as a mother hen gathers her chicks.

Claudia was present at the service as usual, and Onesimus was smitten—as usual. Again, he and she maneuvered the placing so that at the agape meal they sat together. They were careful to include Julius because, as he had said, there weren't many in his age group there.

Claudia's business was thriving, so she kept busy. Yet she and Onesimus walked for a while in the late afternoon and early evening. Julius was youthfully wise enough to plead a reading assignment and left them to themselves.

Onesimus used their time alone to talk on a personal level with Claudia.

"I apologize for my being so forward and overly aggressive several years ago. I wanted you so much, and I wanted you to know of my love."

"I was honored after I recovered from my initial surprise and fright. I cared deeply for you and missed you while you were gone. Now we are both more mature and can allow our friendship to develop as it will."

"I am finding my new place in the household, and you are managing your business well. We are probably the most fortunate couple in Colossae."

Philemon sent a note to Archippus early in the week:

Dear brother, beloved in the Lord, Greeting.

I trust that you are well and all of your household, including the church that meets in your house. I remember our friendship and thank God for you. I plan to visit with the church there on next Lord's Day. Peace to you.

Philemon.

Archippus read the note with an inner chuckle.

"He wants to see what I've done with Onesimus. He's not fooling me. Yet, I will be glad to talk with him and to have him speak to the church—especially since I've given Onesimus his freedom. I really do thank him for encouraging me to 'fulfill my ministry' as Paul described it."

The week was busy. A few of the sheep succumbed to an unknown malady, and Archippus was busy marshalling his shepherds so that all his flocks might be watched closely. Onesimus was involved, both as a messenger and a minister —to the sheep. He was not afraid to do the dirty work necessary. Archippus noted that.

In the midst of Archippus' concern for the animals he decided to ask Onesimus to serve as worship leader on the following Sunday. Archippus had confidence in his former slave's ability and in his willingness. Further he planned to take secret delight in Philemon's reaction—from slave to servant!

On late Saturday afternoon Philemon and some friends from Laodicea arrived. Archippus welcomed them as his guests. Poppae had prepared a meal, and the group gathered in the dining area. Philemon learned quickly that

Onesimus had been granted his freedom. He carefully congratulated Archippus on his generous action and then enthusiastically greeted Onesimus as a freedman. Others from Laodicea remembered Onesimus as a slave in the household and were glad to see him again. Onesimus felt ill at ease with these friends from his past, a feeling he shared in conversation with Julius that night.

"I'm not unconscious as to my years as a slave. But I was not born a slave. Those years were an interruption of my freedom."

"That's true, Onesimus, but I would never have known you except for your slavery—nor would Claudia, nor Poppae."

"I know that, and I'm grateful for you friends—well, for Claudia and Poppae at least."

At the intended omission Julius punched Onesimus on the shoulder, and a brief scuffle resulted.

"I wish my parents had known Paul and Timothy and Luke and Epaphras and Claudia and Poppae—and even you. They were good folks and certainly didn't deserve brutal deaths. I'm not complaining, just reminiscing."

"In the same way I miss my mother, but my father has tried to make up for her absence."

The two young men rarely spoke so seriously with one another. Sleep came quickly.

Again on Sunday the group began to gather. This time Onesimus was a bit anxious. He would be the worship leader and was conscious not only of his friends in Colossae, but also of the visitors from Laodicea, including Philemon. He sensed the respect Archippus felt for Philemon and shared in it. The music began, a low humming at first. Then words came to be recognizable:

> *O praise the Lord, all ye nations;*
> *Laud him, all ye peoples.*
> *For his lovingkindness is great toward us;*
> *And the truth of the Lord endureth forever.*
> *Praise ye the Lord.*

It was a beautiful little psalm. Onesimus sensed rather than saw that Claudia was leading the music. He responded by leading in prayer. Then someone read several paragraphs from the prophet Isaiah that begins "Comfort ye, comfort ye my people" and concludes "the word of our God shall stand forever."

The group expressed concern for one of the faithful members, Lois, who was ill, and voiced prayers for her healing. The service was friendly but orderly. Onesimus presented Philemon and his party, and the group breathed a heartfelt welcome. He then indicated that Philemon would bring the lesson from the Scriptures.

To say that Philemon was overwhelmed by the calm confidence of Onesimus was an understatement. He had seen him a short time before, as a young slave about to be returned to his owner, insecure and frightened at what his master might do. Now the transformation could only be charged to the consideration of Archippus and the cordiality of the church. Archippus too was proud of Onesimus. He recognized that the young man's stay in Ephesus and the ministry of Paul were primarily responsible for his maturity, but this recognition did not lessen his pride in his "son."

It was Philemon who later in the evening talked with Archippus about Onesimus.

"It's amazing. The young man is capable and not at all proud. The church appears to respect and love him. How much training does he have? How old is he? What about his family? What does Paul think of him?"

"You are quite right about the ability of Onesimus and the church's appreciation of his gifts. In response to your questions, he has minimal training of which I am aware. He has gifts for teaching that he has demonstrated with my son. He learned a great many things from Paul. He is 19 years old. I never knew his parents. They were killed in a burglary before I purchased him. Paul's estimate of Onesimus is best noted in his letter."

"Yes, I read that letter before I forwarded it to you. I felt for you as I read it. It certainly put you under pressure to free the young man. Paul must think highly of him to write that sort of letter."

"I trust Paul's appraisal of his worth. Onesimus means 'profitable,' and he has proved profitable to me and to Paul."

"Have you talked with him about his hopes and dreams—his plans?"

"No, not really. He has been so careful since his return, so grateful for his freedom."

"Let's talk to Onesimus."

15

Archippus and Philemon called Onesimus in that very day. The younger man approached the two older ones with respect and some degree of uncertainty. Philemon began the conversation.

"Onesimus, you did well as worship leader last evening. Archippus and I have been talking about you and your plans for the future. Then we decided we probably ought to include you in our discussion of your future."

"I'm so grateful to be included in the household again—especially as a freed man—that I have thought rarely of the future."

"What would you like to do with your life? Rather, what do you think God wants you to do with your life?"

"I want to serve the Lord Christ. If I can do it here, then I shall be happy to minister in Colossae."

"But what about training? You know the resources of Philemon and Archippus are somewhat limited."

"I once dreamed of attending lectures at the University of Tarsus. My father was a student there. Paul studied at Tarsus before going to Gamaliel in Jerusalem. It is an Hellenic school, but I'm not a Jew, and that would probably be a good place for me to get grounded in literature, the arts, philosophy, and economics. I want to be able to communicate with men and women who think and plan and lead."

Archippus responded positively but with caution.

"The University of Tarsus is a reputable school. It does not have the reputation of Athens and Alexandria, however, and is somewhat provincial in appeal. But Strabo certainly was enthusiastic about it, and his friend Athenodorus offered excellent leadership."

In something of an embarrassed state Onesimus seemed to shrug off the prospects of an education.

"That is way off in the future. I shall have to earn and save some money before I can go away to Tarsus."

Archippus reassured him, while adding some humor to the discussion.

"Oh, I have some business friends there—involved in the weaving of goat's hair. That is where Paul learned his trade. You might find part-time employment there. I have some extra funds with which I could make a gift to one or two lecturers. I'm sure we can arrange something. In any event, this household might benefit from your absence. It would certainly be calmer."

Onesimus shared in the good humor but thought there might have been some truth in the statement. He would not be attracted to a situation that was so calm as to appear dead. They all knew that. He had heard of some struggle in Tarsus between the town and the gown. The university exercised a great deal of influence over the city government, and some of the rabble-rousers—especially the gang of Boethus—had resisted this influence. His hopes soared as they continued to talk. Archippus was discussing the issue much as his father might have done. Philemon joined in as a proud uncle.

And so, it was decided that Onesimus would go to Tarsus and investigate the possibilities. Julius was disappointed, but he was becoming involved in his dad's business interests while trying to keep up with his tutor's assignments. Archippus corresponded with textile interests in Tarsus and was able to arrange for housing.

Several months passed. Julius and Onesimus enjoyed their household tasks and church relationships, but they enjoyed being with Claudia more. Indeed, the threesome might have slowed down the courtship between Claudia and Onesimus had it not been for their genuine affection for Julius.

Claudia's business interests were growing, and she became an influential tradeswoman. She too dreaded the day Onesimus would begin his studies in Tarsus. Yet she was proud of his determination to prepare himself for Christian ministry. Poppae looked on proudly while managing to provide tasty food for the household.

Claudia and Onesimus agreed to wait until he had begun his work in Tarsus to announce their plans. They had grown up together and loved one another. They were free and intended to marry. Onesimus knew of Paul's opposition to marriage:

"You ought to remain in the state in which the Lord called you. If you are married, well and good (he meant bad, bad, bad). If you are not married, remain free as I am."

Onesimus had heard it more than once, but he and Claudia decided that the apostle was wrong in his judgment. Meanwhile, Paul was traveling in the Illyricum region.

Parting was sad, but both—yes, all three, Julius included—had come to terms with the separation.

"Claudia, I'm going to the university with mixed feelings. I feel an obligation to prepare for my ministry, but I'll miss you every day and . . . Julius perhaps once a month."

Julius was not present to hear the couple's goodbyes. He would have found hope in Claudia's response.

"I am enjoying my business as you know, but these last few months have convinced me that there's more to my life than dyeing wool. I love you and look forward to your return. This is an interruption . . ."

". . . but only an interruption. Life with you looms ahead—for all of our future."

A warm embrace . . . and Onesimus turned toward Tarsus.

Onesimus took a minimum of personal belongings, knowing he could arrange for his needs in Tarsus. He passed through Lystra and sought out the site of his home and his parents' shop. The scene had changed completely. He looked around for old friends but found none.

"Does anyone remember Prochorus and Porphyra? They kept a little jewelry shop downtown. They had a son named Onesimus."

No one seemed to remember. It was as if that chapter of his life had been closed. He rode on toward Tarsus.

Paul described Tarsus as "no mean city." Indeed, it was not. Capital of the Roman province of Cilicia, it had been the site of Cicero's proconsulship. Both Julius Caesar and Mark Antony had favored it. According to tradition, it was in this vicinity that Antony and Cleopatra met. Its people were cultured and its leadership educated. Most of the students in its university were natives: few came from outside to study there. It was a textile center, with linen woven from the flax grown there. Tents were made from goat's hair—as Paul knew quite well.

North of Tarsus, some 30 miles, loomed Mount Taurus, a long range crossed by travelers through the Cilician Gates. The road turned sharply south for this passage. Onesimus left the wide central plateau and made his way through the natural pass. As the traffic picked up, he sensed that he was nearing Tarsus. East of Tarsus two trade routes joined and had become one for his route.

The road descended south of the mountains even as the river Cydnus splashed sharply downward. He tested its waters and discovered that they were not only swift but also cold—straight from the snowy heights. The river flowed through the center of Tarsus. He saw that it was wide and a central feature of the city, built on its banks. The river plunged in toward the sea, some 10 miles south.

With little trouble Onesimus found the house of a business associate with Archippus. He too was involved with sheep and goats—with wool and hair.

"My name is Onesimus. You have had some correspondence with my good friend, Archippus."

The heavy-set, clearly competent, certainly confident, businessman interrupted him.

"Of course, Onesimus. My name is Heraclides. I've been looking forward to meeting you. You have a place to stay here, thanks to Archippus and our friendship. You also have a place to work if you have time from your studies. Indeed, from what Archippus has written, we might just keep you in Tarsus and set you up in business."

Surprised at the long speech, Onesimus could only mutter his thanks. There would be time for conversation later.

Arrangements were partially made for Onesimus to identify with a peripatetic philosopher and later to study in a more settled atmosphere. He plunged into his studies, listening, reading, and rephrasing his thoughts in written form.

As he had thought, Stoicism was the most popular philosophy in Tarsus. Paul, though not a Stoic, had drunk at the fount of Stoic philosophy. The cosmopolitan nature of Stoicism taught that all men were brothers; that distinction of race and national origin must be abolished.

His teacher and fellow students received Onesimus immediately and warmly. He was grateful for their tolerance of his faith. They would compromise with him. Could he compromise with them? He was equally impressed with their high moral standards and their self-control. They were a virtuous group.

Onesimus found also that all of Tarsus was interested in learning. Not only was the city a philosophy center with tendencies toward Stoicism, but it also boasted of both knowledge and skill in arithmetic and astronomy. Rhetoric complemented its interest in logic and literature. Onesimus, for the first time released in the great flow of learning and living, responded enthusiastically.

He was able to understand some of Paul's independence, something of the apostle's controlled strength. Onesimus thought for himself and compared his Christian faith to the principles of Stoicism. He found some concepts in common, but many more differences. He imagined that his faith completed the goals of Stoicism just as it appeared to complete the goals of Judaism. His own faith became stronger as he confronted new ideas and contrary philosophies.

The year was all too short. Onesimus longed to return to Colossae and to Claudia. He had found some time to work with Heraclides and found him not too demanding. The younger man now spoke more comfortably than at first, and the older responded positively.

"Thank you for your ample provision and your patience."

"Onesimus, the position in this business is open. You are welcome to remain in Tarsus. Invite your friend, Claudia, and make your home here."

There was no temptation to remain, and they parted good friends.

So, with more new thoughts than recently acquired possessions, Onesimus began his return journey. He realized as he made his way back through Galatia and Lystra that his loyalties lay with Asia rather than with his native Galatia. He did not delay his journey even by looking up the churches in Derbe, Lystra, and Iconium. He had matured in the year of separation. There had been a few letters moving back and forth. He was sure of the friendship of Archippus and Julius and of Claudia's love. At age 21 he approached the decisions of adulthood.

And at 21 he approached Colossae. This approach from the east was quite different from the earlier one—with no recent images of a shattered shop and murdered parents and his condition of slavery. It had been a long journey from Tarsus. Both man and beast were weary, though the man had spared the beast as much as his anxiety to see Claudia would allow. He went first to the home of Archippus, his home, and reported to him. Archippus, Julius, and Poppae were beside themselves. It was as if the prodigal had returned. Archippus spoke first.

"Onesimus, how we have missed you! The household has been all too quiet. I hope you have learned enough to teach us arithmetic, astronomy, rhetoric, philosophy, and . . ."

"Ah, sir, don't get your hopes up. I have a great deal of processing to do. Never have I been exposed to so much learning. Never had I known people who loved learning so much."

"We tried to get Claudia to come to the house when we received word that you were to return."

Julius joined in the welcome.

"But she indicated that she had some little beasties ready to boil for that purple dye, and she just couldn't be here."

This called for a good-natured cuff, and Julius was on the receiving end. It was a bit firmer than formerly, but Julius knew himself to be a bit firmer as well.

Poppae simply fell on his shoulder and in his arms . . . this was one of her boys. Almost immediately they adjourned to the kitchen for bread and fruit, always in abundance. Questions drowned out the attempted answers.

Onesimus excused himself and made his way to Claudia's place of business. The greeting was warm and sincere from both young people. It had been a year since they had enjoyed one another's arms. Again, questions drowned out the attempted answers—until Claudia called out.

"Stop! You haven't answered my first questions yet. Do you still love me, or did you find yourself a Tarsian beauty?"

"I'm back, am I not? Do you suppose I would have ridden and walked from Tarsus if I had found anyone there half so beautiful and so good a businesswoman as yourself?"

Enough said! They talked for several hours, then Onesimus went to her home for the evening meal: bread, fruit, and fish—and some vegetables he couldn't identify.

"I never know what you cook, but it's always good."

They talked over their plans.

"Onesimus, what are you going to do? You are equipped to teach, and there are always openings. My business is thriving. We certainly ought not have any financial problems."

"I have not talked about those plans with Archippus yet. I think we owe it to him to include him in them."

Claudia agreed and then added, much later than she had originally intended, a word of almost caution.

"Did Archippus tell you of Paul's recent letter?"

Onesimus had almost forgotten about Paul in his enthusiasm for coming home.

"No, where is he? How is he? What did he write?"

"He's planning a visit perhaps in a month. If you'll remember, he indicated in the letter concerning you that he hoped to visit us here. We felt that it was implied pressure to get Archippus to free you, and perhaps it was—but he knows that you are free and he knows that you have spent a year in Tarsus and he is coming. You know I have never met him."

"Well, you know that he doesn't like women."

"I know nothing of the kind. He thinks a great deal of Lydia, and Lydia thinks a great deal of him."

"Oh, perhaps you will pass the test and be acceptable to him."

"In any event, I'm looking forward to meeting him and hearing him teach. He wrote that his work in Illyricum is completed and he hopes to go to Jerusalem."

"I doubt that he will be received there with open arms, but he is absolutely fearless."

At this point they said their goodbyes and Onesimus returned to the house he had come to call his home. There he found the household asleep except for Julius. The young men, separated for a year, hardly ceased talking until daylight. Then, at the time for undertaking the day's business, they suddenly became sleepy.

Excitement kept them both going through the day. Archippus had reserved much of it for a debriefing session with Onesimus.

"Onesimus, son, you have no idea how much we, I, have missed you. Of course, Julius has missed you as well. Were you continually happy with the arrangement—as happy as you seemed to be earlier?"

"You fixed things up for me. I was comfortable in the living quarters, and I found my relations with the lecturers most challenging."

He did not go into the same sort of detail with Archippus as he had with Julius the night before. Archippus might not have understood.

"I suppose you have heard that Paul is planning to come by for a visit."

"Yes, Claudia told me last night."

"I don't think he's coming to check up on me—but perhaps on you. He knows that you are a free man, and he knows that you have been studying in Tarsus. He'll probably have a thousand questions to ask about that 'no mean city'."

"I look forward to meeting him again. A lot has happened since that riot in Ephesus. I wish he were not planning to go to Jerusalem. They'll clobber him."

"My experience with Paul has been that he's able to take care of himself."

"Now how about you? What would you like to do? How can I help you? Of course, we need you as a leader in the church—still meeting in our house."

"I want to help in the ministry. Indeed, that's my calling."

"Then I can think of no greater challenge than here in Colossae. If our folks were more aggressive in their Christian witness, I'm sure we would face more opposition. As it is, most of the legalists have pulled out of the church and are making noises about organizing a new group of believers. It reminds me of Paul's written statement: 'If we or an angel of heaven should preach to you any gospel other than that which I preached to you, he is to be anathema.' I hardly see how that is possible, but then I'm just a businessman."

"You are much more than 'just a businessman.' You have managed to hold the church together, and it has attracted a great many new folks—or so Julius tells me."

"Julius has matured, has he not? He has taken an active interest in my business. He may be going off to school one of these days. He has missed you! I hope you will stay around long enough to renew your friendship. Indeed, I hope you will give serious consideration to taking an active role in leading the church. This is your home for as long as you will stay."

Onesimus was somewhat overcome by the warmth of Archippus.

"I think you ought to know that Claudia and I are talking of marriage. Colossae has become her home even as it has become mine. Her business is increasing, thanks to your encouragement and backing. I can teach, and together we can make a living that will allow both of us to assume responsibilities in the church. You have been generous with it, and I hope you will yet permit it to meet in your house."

Archippus had some difficulty breaking in on Onesimus.

"Congratulations. I know that you and Claudia have loved one another for several years. I feel like a father to you both and would like nothing better than to provide the wedding feast and assume all other expenses."

Again, Onesimus was overwhelmed. The days of his master's sharp rebukes faded into the distant past. The Christian faith had made a great difference. Archippus interrupted the brief silence.

"We need to make preparations for Paul's visit. Perhaps the wedding plans could coincide with his coming."

Onesimus sensed how Paul would react to a prospective church leader planning to get married but held his peace for the time being.

News of Onesimus' return spread rapidly through Colossae. By the weekend all of the church anticipated his presence. He felt a bit uneasy, however, as Archippus planned to recommend him for leadership. He knew something of the state of affairs: the departure of the legalists had certainly promoted the peace of the group, but they had not been fully replaced by newer members. The church needed firm, full-time planning.

Sunday afternoon saw a larger than normal attendance, and Onesimus quickly responded to the warm worship. He and Claudia had agreed to announce their betrothal at the agape feast following worship. Everyone was excited about their decision and also looked forward to the new relation with Onesimus as responsible leader. When Archippus also announced that Paul was coming for a visit their enthusiasm reached a new high.

Onesimus gathered a small group of young men about him—their parents were eager for them to study with him. Archippus, Onesimus, and Julius decided that Julius ought to maintain his present arrangements. Perhaps the two friends were so close as to make learning difficult.

Archippus arranged a large room at his business headquarters for teaching purposes, which occupied Onesimus' mornings. His relationship with the students and their families complemented other relationships he was cultivating with Archippus' business friends. These, along with Claudia's business clients, expanded the influence of Onesimus and enhanced the reputation of the church in Colossae. Those who had severed relationships with the church looked on in a potentially dangerous jealousy.

16

Paul was coming. Onesimus and Claudia were making wedding plans. The church was ecstatic.

Paul followed his usual itinerary: Ephesus to Laodicea to Colossae. He was clearly headed for Jerusalem and would probably go to Miletus to board a ship. Yet, he had longed to visit Colossae, especially now that Archippus had been reconciled with Onesimus. He had also heard about Onesimus' year in Tarsus. A great many questions teased him toward Colossae.

Paul arrived in the middle of the week, greeted warmly by Archippus and Onesimus. The apostle jokingly inquired about their relationship, to which the older man and then the younger responded.

"A slave or a brother beloved?"

"Neither: the relationship is that of father and son."

"That's even better. I know you two were made for each other."

"Re-made . . . Your kindness toward me in Ephesus made it possible."

"Let's ascribe the entire miracle to the grace of God!"

Conversation continued late into the night, began early in the morning, and filled the day. Onesimus and Paul had many interests in common. Julius and Archippus may have been neglected. Paul was impressed with Claudia, but not enthusiastic about the wedding plans. He talked with Onesimus about his future.

"You have certain gifts. And your year in Tarsus along with your experience here at Colossae have strengthened their development. Do not underestimate your contribution during the months at Ephesus. I am glad that you have gathered a class of young men whom you are teaching. This will strengthen your ministry in the church. Archippus tells me he is grooming you for leadership here at Colossae. Count on me as a good friend if I can help."

"You certainly can help. For example, we want you to lead in worship and teaching this weekend. It's a rare treat for any church to hear you. It will be your first visit to Colossae."

"I shall be honored and glad to speak Sunday. I've been working on some ideas about the relationship between Christ and the church. Perhaps I can explore those in my homily."

An even larger group greeted Paul on the next Sunday afternoon. He spoke first of his own experience, beginning with a brief account of his confrontation with the Lord on the road to Damascus.

"He charged me to go to the Gentiles, and I have not been disobedient to the heavenly vision. Of course, I have great love for my own nation. I have on most visits to new places begun with a visit to the synagogue. I hope to talk with Jewish kinsmen during this stay in Colossae."

He talked of his most recent work in Illyricum.

"I am always challenged by those placed where the gospel has not been preached. We were able to establish some church groups there."

He then began to talk of a recent project.

"You know that I am going to Jerusalem. I want to go as a representative of the Gentile churches. Famine has caused intense suffering, especially among Jewish Christians. Gentile churches have been generous with gifts I will take to Jerusalem. Other representatives of Gentile churches will accompany me from Miletus to Jerusalem. This ought to go a long way toward softening any hard feelings about my Gentile ministry."

He hesitated before receiving a question from a concerned believer.

"Won't you be in great danger in Jerusalem? We have heard that the feeling against Gentiles is so great there that you will be risking your life."

Paul replied in characteristic fashion.

"I have no fear of giving my life for the sake of the gospel."

He then took a different tack, speaking forcefully against the so-called Colossian heresy.

"I understand there has been trouble here in the church, and that some have stopped attending these services, preferring an emphasis on the necessity of obeying the Law."

Some of those had returned to hear Paul, the exponent of God's grace.

"Let me remind you that the prophets thundered forth against Israel's fasts and feasts and that our Lord himself used the Sabbath as a day of ministry. This day is as every day, except that we gather for worship. And our Lord is pre-eminent. The Law or angels cannot compete with him. God has spoken finally, completely in him. It is for us to fill up in our own suffering that which is lacking for the sake of the church."

Some members of the congregation were writhing at this straightforward talk. Some vowed to themselves that Paul couldn't get by with it. Paul sensed their hostility, as did Archippus, Onesimus, and others.

No one was really surprised then the next day when two magistrates showed up at the house of Archippus with an order for Paul's house arrest because of stirring up trouble in a peaceful community. The terms of the sentence were not too troublesome: Paul could communicate with the church since it was meeting in the house. Nevertheless, he resented the charge and resisted the sentence. Both Archippus and Onesimus sought to calm him down.

Plans for the wedding of Claudia and Onesimus continued. Because Philemon in Laodicea knew both of them better than Paul, Claudia liked the idea of his pronouncing the benediction and presiding at the wedding feast. Paul would certainly be an honored guest, though they were not at all certain as to his position regarding the marriage. Because there were no parents in evidence on either side—Onesimus' had been killed and Claudia's had long since disappeared—Archippus made all the arrangements. Since both had been his slaves, he had a father's interest in the match.

The wedding feast would take place at the home of Archippus, and he also had insisted that the newly-married couple make their home with him until they could find a house of their own.

The wedding day arrived. Claudia was busily preparing herself at her house. She bathed, anointed her body with perfume, and dressed in white linen. At the appointed time Onesimus arrived in a chariot provided for the occasion. Friends accompanied him on horseback and made a procession back to the house of Archippus.

Julius especially enjoyed the activity. Both Claudia and Onesimus were his dear friends. It was a period of great joy. Only Paul may have been fuming, but he sought to hide it. After all, he was under house arrest—which might have limited his joyous response.

When the couple and their attendants returned to the house of Archippus, almost all of the church waited. They welcomed the bride and the groom—friends of both. Philemon ceremoniously welcomed them and began the blessing on their union:

> *Blessed be the God and Father of our Lord Jesus Christ, who has blessed us with every spiritual blessing in the heavenly placed in Christ Jesus.*
> *And blessed be the remembrance of our Lord's life in the flesh, who loved us and gave himself for us.*

> *And blessed be those for whom he died—men and women, boys and girls—made in the image of their Heavenly Father.*
>
> *And blessed be the love that draws them to one another—the man to the woman and the woman to the man.*
>
> *And blessed be the feast at which they are united as husband and wife.*
>
> *And blessed be the home that is established in Christ and founded in the love he has for his church.*
>
> *And blessed be your children, Onesimus and Claudia, and their children, and their children's children. Amen.*

Throughout the benediction and words of explanation Onesimus and Claudia stood silent and prayerful. With the exultant "Amen!" of the guests they too came alive in joyful acceptance of many good wishes. The feast, supervised by none other than loving Poppae, was an event of several days. It seemed that all of Colossae attended.

Finally, the last wedding feast guests had departed, leaving Archippus, Julius, Onesimus, Claudia, and Paul alone. All were ready for a calmer context.

"Do you remember that we have a story about Jesus and his disciples attending a wedding feast?" asked Paul.

"Yes, and he made water into wine," added Julius.

"Well, our wine did not run out and everyone appeared to enjoy the festivities."

Archippus took satisfaction in the job well done.

At the first opportunity Paul, who was becoming somewhat stir crazy with his house restraint, cornered Onesimus.

"Don't forget that your primary loyalties are to the Lord and his church. You have certain gifts, entrusted to you for development. You have a great opportunity here in Colossae. You have an overwhelming responsibility for the church. Now that you are married, your ministry is limited. You will be trying to please your wife and not the Lord."

Onesimus interrupted sharply.

"Not so! Claudia and I both will be trying to please the Lord—and we can do it better together. You'll see."

Paul sensed the younger man's resentment and began to talk of his plans for continuing house arrest.

"I'm not sure how long I'll be here, but I want to write a bit—perhaps in honor of the wedding celebration."

"We would be grateful for that, but you have so many concerns, so many church relationships."

"Not one of which I can satisfy so long as Colossae's magistrates believe my accusers. I need to be on my way to Jerusalem."

Onesimus sensed that the conversation had run its course and excused himself. Archippus had provided Paul a large room, and he was comfortable in his house arrest. The apostle called Onesimus back just as he was going out the door.

"I wonder, Onesimus, if I could get some more 'profit' out of you. Your parents did not name you in vain. I do want to write a letter to the Christians of Asia, and I need some help in the writing."

Onesimus responded quickly with affirmation.

"I would be honored to assist in any way I can . . . if I may depend on you to assist in our worship from Sunday to Sunday—or as long as you are here . . ."

"I trust that will not be much longer, which suggests something of my haste to undertake the letter. I'm ready to begin now—here and now."

"Wait until I can get ink and paper. I'll go to the office."

He moved out with new dignity, a responsible scribe-to-be. In a moment he returned and sat behind the desk, pen poised and paper ready. Paul laughed at the sight of the young man in all his dignity. He walked across the room and then back again.

"Paul, apostle of Christ Jesus . . ."

"I refuse to dignify this house arrest by describing myself as a prisoner. I am an apostle, the least and the last to be sure, but apostle nonetheless."

Onesimus wrote on, then became conscious of the fact that Paul had interrupted the dictating process. With a bit of embarrassment, he ceased writing until he was certain Paul was "writing" again.

". . . apostle of Christ Jesus through God's will to the saints who are . . ."

"Leave that blank and we'll personalize copies to Laodicea, Hierapolis, Ephesus, and the rest."

". . . to the saints and faithful folks in Christ Jesus. Grace to you and peace from God our Father and Lord Jesus Christ."

"When I leave for Miletus I will take copies of the letter, one for Miletus, and one for Ephesus. Then, if you will fill in the blank for these cities in the Lycus Valley . . ."

Again, Onesimus continued writing until he realized that Paul was making conversation. Little wonder that Paul's letters were so treasured: it was as if Paul himself was speaking when they were read.

"Blessed be God, even Father of our Lord Jesus Christ, he who blessed us with every spiritual blessing in the heavenly places in Christ."

Any difficulties Paul and Onesimus might have suspected in the matter of the recent marriage disappeared in the closeness of the two now, utterly committed to writing a letter. Onesimus had learned the value of the apostle's writing.

They took a brief break for lunch and enjoyed the light meal Poppae had prepared. She had delighted in providing the wedding feast but seemed to revert naturally to the warmth of the smaller household meal. Soon Paul became restive and Onesimus followed him back to their writing laboratory. For several hours they worked: Paul repeating and rephrasing, Onesimus correcting. He sensed that they were nearing the end.

". . . speaking to one another in psalms and hymns and spiritual songs, singing and praising the Lord in your hearts, giving thanks always for all people in the name of our Lord Jesus Christ—giving thanks to God, even the Father, submitting yourselves to one another in the fear of Christ."

"Enough!" declared Paul.

Onesimus had difficulty keeping up with Paul's almost limitless clauses and phrases. His grammar was perfect, but quite involved. One sentence earlier had taken an entire page. He remembered that Paul had indicated he might write something in honor of the wedding. This did not appear to be that kind of letter, so Onesimus decided not to ask about it. Once again he excused himself, and Paul thanked him for his help. It was in the early evening before the newlyweds had an opportunity to talk.

Claudia had been occupied with the purple-dyeing business, growing rapidly under her efficient management and the referrals of Archippus. She and Onesimus reported on their days. She was especially interested in the letter Paul had written.

Almost as soon as Onesimus left the room, Paul, yet alert and ready to write, took up the pen and continued the letter:

"submitting yourselves to one another in the fear of Christ . . . Wives to your own husbands as to the Lord . . ."

"Now I'm not an authority on that subject, but I sense a comparison here: I do know of a relationship between Christ and the church."

". . . because as the husband is head of the wife, so also Christ is the head of the church, being himself savior of the body. But as the church submits herself to Christ, so also wives to their husbands in everything . . ."

"Wait a moment. I want to emphasize that the marriage relationship is one of mutual submissiveness. He reread the phrase "submitting yourselves to one another in the fear of Christ."

"That's what I mean—to one another. How can I develop that idea? How about this?"

"Husbands, love your wives, just as Christ loved the church and gave himself for it . . . so husbands ought to love their own wives as their own bodies. The one loving his own wife loves himself."

Paul seemed satisfied with this word. He remembered the first time he had met Julius and Onesimus, a rebel duo. Good-naturedly he turned to children and their relationship with their parents:

"Children, obey your parents in the Lord . . ."

Was the word "obey" better than "submit"? Yes, he decided. It's a different relationship. But he added a word of caution.

"And you fathers, do not provoke your children, but nurture them in the training and instruction of the Lord."

The next paragraph followed naturally—from the experience of Onesimus to the institution of slavery.

"You slaves, obey your masters according to the flesh in fear and trembling . . . and you masters, treat your slaves in the same way . . ."

He reread the paragraphs and felt they applied the principle of mutual submissiveness he had stated, "submitting yourselves to one another in the fear of Christ." Three areas had been touched: husbands and wives, children and parents, and masters and slaves.

Enough for the evening. He felt that this comment on household relationships would serve to direct the letter in honor of the marriage of two friends, loving children: Onesimus and Claudia.

Early the next morning two uniformed legionnaires presented themselves at the house of Archippus. Paul caught sight of them. He imagined them in combat and felt a homily coming on . . . a belt of truth, a breastplate of righteousness, sandals of readiness, shield of faith . . . Even as they summoned a servant to the door, Paul knew how his letter would end.

As it turned out, they came from the magistrate to lift the house arrest. Paul and his friends could hardly contain themselves. He immediately began to make plans to journey toward Miletus and Jerusalem. His letter?

"Onesimus, will you help me complete the letter?"

"I thought we had finished it."

"No, I have one or two paragraphs to write."

And so Onesimus, not noticing the extra page Paul had added, began again.

"For the rest, be strong in the Lord and in the power of his might. Put on the whole armor of God . . ."

Paul was ready to conclude the letter with an appeal for the church to deal realistically with the problems of evil in a hostile world. When he mentioned Tychicus, Onesimus perked up. Then Paul explained his reason for including the former.

"You and Claudia are going to be busy here, and someone needs to take copies of the letter to the churches. Tychicus will be here to accompany me to Miletus. He will know about my affairs."

Paul added a benediction and asked Onesimus to enlist help for the copying process. Julius, Archippus, and Claudia worked with Onesimus. Only in the copying did Onesimus and Claudia recognize the reference to the home—this newly established home—with its relationships. They were overcome at the approval the letter spelled out.

17

Claudia and Onesimus did not see Paul again. They heard reports and on occasion received greetings from him through Timothy, Tychicus, and others. They wrote to Paul, reporting on the work at Colossae. Meanwhile Julius had reached the age when he and his father began to talk about advanced schooling. His horizons were limited in Colossae. Several possibilities presented themselves.

Julius expressed an interest in Tarsus, largely because Onesimus had been happy with his experience there. Onesimus tried to dissuade him and partly succeeded. He was financially able to further his education in either Alexandria or Athens. The cosmopolitan nature of Athens won the day.

Julius made his plans and went to Athens, unsure of what he would do afterward. While there, although he diligently seized the opportunities for study Athens afforded, he was drawn back to Colossae and Archippus, Onesimus and Claudia. So, after a year he returned to join his father in business and his good friends as a lay leader in the church.

By this time Paul was known to be under arrest in Caesarea. He was destined for Rome and then Spain. Soon thereafter he was arrested again and executed under Emperor Nero's authority.

For several years Onesimus ministered faithfully to the church and community in Colossae. The church grew stronger with the added help of Julius, now a mature young man.

The work at Ephesus eclipsed other Asian churches. Hierapolis, Laodicea, and even Colossae were not able to reach out to the province as effectively as the church in the capital city. The church at Ephesus sent a letter to Onesimus seeking his help:

> *Onesimus, we know about your work at Colossae, and we remember you as a young man here in Ephesus. We believe this is a strategic church in the province. We do not look down on your work there in Colossae. We would encourage you to consider moving with Claudia to our city and to become the leader of this church.*

The letter from Ephesus continued, but Onesimus simply skimmed the other paragraphs. He was overwhelmed by the invitation, but he was not interested in leaving Colossae. The work of the church was expanding, Claudia was active in business, and his friends were in Colossae. Nevertheless, he discussed the invitation with Claudia, who perhaps approached it with more maturity than her husband.

"Do you suppose we ought to consider this?"

"This may be a good opportunity to minister. You know this is our life, and we have had no assurance that we would spend our lives in Colossae."

"But your business, Claudia . . . it does seem that things have worked out for us to be permanent here."

"There is no permanence in places. You ought to know that from Paul's experience. He has ministered all over the empire."

"But I'm not Paul, and Paul is not married."

Claudia reminded him sharply of an earlier conversation.

"Do you remember how we told Paul before we married that neither of us would allow our marriage to interfere with our Christian vocation?"

Onesimus remembered.

So, Onesimus and Claudia decided to leave Colossae, much to the regret of the church and their friends there. He tried to reassure Julius and Archippus of a continued relationship.

"Ephesus is not so far. You can arrange business trips in that direction. And perhaps you will invite us back for a visit or for a church responsibility."

Reluctantly Archippus contacted friends in Ephesus who would insure business opportunities for Claudia in her purple-dye sales.

As the couple prepared to leave, Archippus called out to Onesimus.

"Wait. I have something I want to give to you. It really is yours by all rights."

Archippus had kept it for several years in a leather case in his office. Now he opened the case and gave both the case and its contents to Onesimus. It was the letter Paul had addressed to Archippus by way of Philemon, requesting freedom for the slave.

Onesimus shed tears at that. All of his former master's patience and all of his foster-father's love came to a focal point in the gift. They embraced as father and son, as did Onesimus and Julius—brothers.

The ministry in Ephesus was difficult and not always appreciated as had been the work in the smaller city. Paul had not won the struggle against Artemis and her priests and priestesses, and neither could Onesimus. It was deeply entrenched.

From time to time Julius and Archippus and friends from Colossae and Laodicea visited in Ephesus. Many other believers passed through the capital city. Some came from Galatia and others from Corinth, Philippi, and Thessalonica. They too had known Paul, and Paul had written letters to the churches of which they were members.

One day after they had lived in Ephesus for many years, Onesimus presented an idea to Claudia regarding the work of Paul.

"Our friend Paul has written so many letters, some of which we have seen. But Paul has long since gone to his reward and these letters might be lost, even though each church treasures its own letter. Why don't we ask the churches we know to have letters to share a copy with us? Then, with my letter as a beginning, we can collect copies of the others and insure their safety."

Claudia thought the idea a good one, so she began the process. Of course, the church in Ephesus had a copy of the letter Paul had written from Colossae—and so did Onesimus and Claudia. And Onesimus had the letter concerning his freedom. Claudia wrote to the church at Corinth and was surprised some time later to receive copies of four letters addressed by Paul to that church. She also wrote to Philippi and to Thessalonica and received copies of their letters. Onesimus had no trouble with the letter sent to Colossae. A request addressed to Lystra was rewarded by a letter Paul had written to the Galatians.

Soon a report reached them that Paul had written a letter to Rome—many years before, and even before he had visited the city or the church. An inquiry verified the existence of a letter to the Romans. Of course, they were willing to share a copy. Others heard of the project and supplied letters—some clearly not genuine.

Some standards for genuineness had to be established. Everyone sought to get in on the act. Letters written to individuals tended to resemble the one written to Archippus. Neither Onesimus nor Claudia wanted to run the risk of losing a genuine letter from Paul. There was no list to guide them. They did all in their power to protect their treasure.

So, while Onesimus was pastor at Ephesus the collection of Paul's letters came into being—all because a returning slave had been protected by a letter from Ephesus by way of Laodicea to Colossae.

"See that you read the letter from Laodicea. And say to Archippus, 'Look out for the ministry that you have received in the Lord, that you fulfill it'."

A few years later Onesimus would receive a letter as leader of the church, a letter written to the church at Ephesus by one Ignatius. Admittedly the letter referred to Onesimus as pastor and thanked him for visiting the writer in prison—shades of the past!

CPSIA information can be obtained
at www.ICGtesting.com
Printed in the USA
FFHW022334011218
49723882-54160FF